BOOK CLUB

An Evening at Franc's

Jeannette Dashiell

Registered WGA

DEDICATION

Sometimes
Amid your darkest nightmare,
Laughter finds you.
Thank you, Hannah.

ACKNOWLEDGMENTS

*T*hank you to my wonderful husband, Dennis, and amazing daughter Maddy for loving, supporting, and believing in me. I love you more than words can express.

Thank you to my family, my friends, and my own book club, BABs (Books and Booze), for encouraging me to write.

A very special thank-you to my twin sister, Jennifer McKay, for starting this journey with me and for her creative input that helped to make this book come to life.

Most importantly, I would like to thank my daughter Hannah, who passed away in a car accident on January 5, 2014. I strive each day to live my life as she lived hers, with enthusiasm, humor, kindness, character, and love. She is my angel watching from above and living within my heart.

To donate to scholarships for young women going into medicine, please visit the Hannah Dashiell Memorial Fund:

www.whatcomcf.org/dashiell-scholarship

CONTENTS

Acknowledgments   v

Prologue Franc's   xi

Part One   **Franc's, Book Club, Derek, and Drinks**   1

Chapter 1   Frances "Franc" Giuliani   3

Chapter 2   Ten Years Earlier: Book Club Is Born   14

Chapter 3   Present Day: Getting Ready for
Book Club   40

Chapter 4   Thursday Morning at Franc's   64

Chapter 5   The Ladies of Book Club
Arrive at Franc's   74

Part Two   **Orders Are Taken**   87

Chapter 6   Sophia's Beauty Advice   89

Chapter 7   Kathy and the Merger   92

Chapter 8   Grandkids   99

Chapter 9   Stanley and Indigestion   102

Chapter 10 Dinner Specials   108
Chapter 11 A Wedding and A Funeral   111
Chapter 12 Relevance and Motherhood   121
Chapter 13 Diane and the Secrets of High Society   130
Chapter 14 Pork and Watermelons   137
Chapter 15 The Confession   147
Chapter 16 Sophia and Roman Working Together   150
Chapter 17 Kathy's Overactive Bladder   154
Chapter 18 Sarah and Loneliness   161

Part Three Dinner Is Served   167
Chapter 19 Dishes Aren't the Only Things
            Hot at Franc's   169
Chapter 20 Bette, Las Vegas, a Man, a Tattoo,
            and a Ring   173
Chapter 21 One Love Story Blossoms While
            Another One Crumbles   183
Chapter 22 Fractured Marriage and A
            White Wedding   198
Chapter 23 Sophia and the Reservation   204
Chapter 24 Ali and Mr. Wonderful   207

Part Four   Desserts, Drinks, and Goodnight   213
Chapter 25 Battle of the Wits   215
Chapter 26 Drinks, Desserts, Heartbreak,
            and Bonding   217
Chapter 27 Melissa Embraces a New Chapter
            in Her Life   230

Chapter 28 Sarah and Charlie   242
Chapter 29 Dating and Whole Foods   250
Chapter 30 Gravity, Surprises, and Realizations   258
Chapter 31 An Evening at Franc's Comes
                to An End   270

About the Author   273

FRANC'S

Her name is Frances, but everyone calls her Franc, and this is her restaurant, *Franc's*. It was named after her grandfather and the business's first owner, Francisco Giuliani Sr. The restaurant is located on Tenth Avenue in Manhattan. It's what the *New York Times* likes to call a modern take on Italian cuisine. Each night at *Franc's*, she has the pleasure to serve a variety of customers, some of whom are more memorable than others and some she feels honored to say have become more like family rather than patrons.

Franc's father, Francisco Giuliani Jr., being from a traditional Italian family, was determined to have a son to carry on his name like the generations before him had done. Already having had four daughters, he was thrilled the day his wife, Sophia, announced she was pregnant again for the fifth and *"final time."* Nine months later, when she blessed him yet again with another daughter, he knew his dream of passing along the family name was over. Aware of how much this tradition meant to her husband, Sophia suggested they name their tiny newborn Frances. Cradling his daughter in his arms for the first time, he looked down at his beautiful baby and called her Franc, a nickname that, to the dismay of her mother, would stick with her forever. This is the legacy Franc has spent her whole life trying to uphold…and, some days, live down.

Tonight is Thursday. For some of you, that means it's close to the end of the workweek, and for some of you lucky ones, this means "book club"—that one night of the month to sit with your friends, rarely discussing the chosen book, and to eat, drink, and, more importantly, share with the group what's been happening in your life. It's a magical night where you shrug off the labels of who you are, a night when you are no one's wife, mother, coworker, or boss. At the book club, you are just *you*, in all your uninhibited glory.

There is an unwritten code that comes along with book club. It is a rule that cannot ever be compromised or broken, no matter how tempting. And that rule is, "What's said at book club stays at book club." This, my friends, is why book club has stood the test of time. Through dating, marriages, divorces, children, jobs won and lost, tragedy, and illness, you will always have your book club. So if you are fortunate enough to be invited in, say yes. Cherish this time spent together with your girlfriends, because you are *one of the lucky ones.*

The book club that gathers tonight at *Franc's* is no different. These ladies have been meeting here for the past ten years. They come together once a month to share their lives as one another's biggest supporters, confidantes, and secret keepers. Over the years, Franc has noticed that their book club has become less and less about the book discussions and more about the unconditional bond of female friendships. While it is still referred to as book club, she hasn't seen them open a book in three years. However, each of them still carries her book with her every month, like a symbolic badge of honor.

PART ONE

Franc's, Book Club, Derek, and Drinks

CHAPTER 1

FRANCES "FRANC" GIULIANI

For most of you, Saturday and Sunday are your days to lounge, but because she is a restaurant owner, Franc's day of relaxation is Tuesday. On those days, she likes to start her mornings off slowly, spending a few quiet minutes curled up in her warm blankets with her iPad, looking over e-mails and catching up on the morning news before heading to the bathroom to splash water on her face and brush her teeth before pulling her hair into a ponytail. Back in her room, Franc throws on a pair of running pants, a sweatshirt, sneakers, and her beloved Mets cap before heading out the door for her weekly run through the park.

The tattered cap is one of the only things she has left from her relationship with Aaron. It was around Franc's thirtieth birthday when her sister, Theresa, set her up on a blind date with a coworker of her husband's. On their first date, Aaron took Franc to see a Mets game. That's where he bought her the baseball cap and when her love affair for the team began. The connection Aaron and she shared was comfortable, and it didn't take long before they decided to find a place of their own. Aaron was what her mom, Sophia, calls "a real catch": smart, kind, handsome, and funny. Everyone loved him—everyone, it seems, except for Franc. She's not sure why. On paper they were the perfect match, and even their parents got along. But as time went on, Franc came to think of him more as a friend than the great love of her life. So when the opportunity came for him to take a promotion in Ohio, she eagerly encouraged him to take it. She had hoped for truth in the old adage "absence makes the heart grow fonder." However, in her case, the only thing that grew was Franc's certainty of her wavering feelings. They struggled along for another year and a half in this long-distance romance before deciding to officially call it quits—a decision her mom has never let her forget. She still refers to him as "the one that got away." Since then Aaron has met and married a wonderful woman named Jen, and they have three sons. Over the years Franc and he have been able to remain good friends and still get together whenever he and his family are in town. The Mets cap is a warm reminder of their special friendship.

With the cap pulled low on her forehead and ear-buds blaring AC/DC, Franc quickly finds her pace on the running trail. On her way home from the park, Franc stops to treat herself to an everything bagel smothered in a thick layer of rich cream cheese from a bakery on Hamlin Street. Walking through the streets of her neighborhood, Franc savors each bite as she makes her way to the floral shop, Bella Flora. The shop's owner, Steven, anticipating her weekly visit, has her bundle of pink peonies wrapped and waiting for her.

When she returns home from her errands, Franc makes her way to the bathroom to wash off the sweat from her morning run. Looking at her reflection in the mirror above the sink as she waits for the water to heat in her shower, she is struck by the wrinkles that have started to creep along the undersides of her eyes and spread from the corners of her mouth. As she runs her index fingers along the trails, tracing the new creases, she questions, "When did this happen?" To make matters worse, after close observation of her now-aging face, she notices the glitter of gray reflecting north of her puffy eyes. Lifting her bangs from her forehead, Franc continues to question the current situation. "And when did this happen?" Reluctantly, she acknowledges that the life of a restaurant owner has begun taking its toll on her once-youthful body. All the late nights and early mornings, invoices and orders, menus and specials, staff management, as well as catering to the egos of the chefs, combine to create the perfect storm now prominently displayed across her face. Why, you ask, does she continue to do this to herself day in and day out? Because, my friends, when the restaurant is buzzing and filled with happy patrons and the kitchen is moving like one organic body, Franc believes there is no better high. That is what she lives for; it is in her genes.

Today, however, it is not a day of relaxation—in fact, quite the contrary, because today is Thursday, one of Franc's busiest days of the week. Like clockwork, Franc wakes moments before her alarm has a chance to do its morning job. In striking contrast to her restaurant, her apartment is modern and sparse. In the corner of her bedroom sits an original Wassily Chair made of chrome and black leather that she bought from a dealer in SoHo. Her king-size bed has a simple ebony head-board and is covered with a quilted, white down com-forter and flanked by two stainless-steel nightstands on either side. One table holds a clear acrylic lamp, topped with a white shade, and a cubic mahogany alarm clock, and on the other sits a matching lamp and a small crys-tal bud vase filled with her favorite flowers, pale-pink peonies that she picked up two days earlier on her day off. The kitchen and living room in her apartment are no different from the bedroom. They are clean and de-cluttered, consisting of only the essentials. At the restau-rant, Franc is constantly surrounded by opulence, color, sound, people, movement, and chaos all day long. So in order to combat this, she has created her personal space to be the opposite. It's a place where her mind and senses can take a break from the continuous bombardment of stimuli, a place where she can take a breath and relax in the beauty of its simplicity.

Franc is the third generation to own and manage the restaurant. Her grandfather Francisco Giuliani opened Franc's in the early sixties. He wasn't a trained chef; instead, he cooked from the heart. He filled *Franc's* with the tastes and aromas he had grown up with as a child. These were the cherished recipes handed down through the generations from his mother and her mother before and so on. As with most Italian families, these recipes are top secret, considered more valuable than gold. However, the one thing that is certain about each of these recipes is that they are all made with love, patience, and the freshest ingredients. When Franc's grandfather came to the United States as a small boy with his family in the late 1930s, his mother brought these beloved recipes with her from the old country. Each one was tucked safely away in her stockings and carefully cradled in her suitcase. When Franc's father, Francisco Giuliani Jr., came of age, he took over as manager and later head chef and eventually owner of the restaurant. This, however, was not before he had spent many years learning all the ins and outs of running and owning the restaurant business and not until her grandfather was convinced her dad could re-create the family recipes successfully on his own.

Franc's childhood was different from other girls' her age because most of it was spent at the restaurant. While most kids were playing chase in the park, the Giuliani sisters had fun playing hide-and-seek in the basement among the pantry items. They learned to play poker with the busboys, while their mother worked in the front of the restaurant as the hostess or in the office where she helped balance the books. It was also the place where Franc had her first taste of alcohol, when she was just twelve years old, from Maxine, the bartender. Maxine snuck her a shot of cherry schnapps while Franc's parents were in the stockroom, taking inventory. She said it would help with Franc's menstrual cramps. Franc doesn't remember it making her cramps go away, but she does remember it made her belly feel warm and her head a little dizzy. A few years later, when she turned fifteen, while other girls her age were going to the movies with their boyfriends, Franc smoked her first cigarette in the alley behind the restaurant with a dishwasher named Antonio. And the following year, while most of her classmates were worried about being asked to the prom, Franc lost her virginity to a waiter named Mario.

Mario was just two years older than Franc. He worked part-time to put himself through his freshman year at the local community college. She remembers thinking that he seemed so worldly and mature. They spent many hours together at the restaurant as he told her all about his dreams and plans for his future. Franc was completely overcome, as only teenage love can do, believing she had found her soul mate. That is, until she stepped into the walk-in freezer and caught him making out with one of the hostesses. It was then that Franc vowed she would never get involved with someone she worked with ever again!

Franc has many memories from over the years of following her parents around, listening to how they interacted with the employees and staff members. Sometimes these exchanges, especially with the chefs, would escalate into something that would make it feel as if the kitchen were shaking. To an outsider, this might have looked frightening, but to the Giulianis, this was normal. Shouting with hotheaded tempers and then making up with the warmth of a family was how they communicated. As with most Italian families, they shouted loudly but loved even louder.

After Franc graduated from high school, her parents made the decision that she should get out of the restaurant and see the world. Truth be told, Sophia didn't want her daughter to follow in her father's and grandfather's footsteps of becoming the chef and owner of *Franc's*. She felt it would be too difficult for Franc to find someone to settle down with and, most importantly, give her lots of grandchildren while being stuck away in a hot kitchen until all hours of the night. Apparently, to her the vision of her youngest daughter wearing a white apron splattered with the daily special and sweat beading on her forehead from the heat coming off the stoves wasn't exactly the most attractive look. After thinking about it for a while, in a way, Franc could see her mom had a point. So with a little persuasion, her parents convinced Franc that she needed to leave New York and expand her horizons. For a complete change of surroundings, they sent her to attend school at Arizona State University to get her business degree. However, being stuck in the desert wasn't exactly what Franc had in mind when her parents said, "See the world." Franc knows her mom was just hoping that while she was away she would find a nice young man to settle down with and forget all about taking over *Franc's* when her dad was ready to retire.

To the dismay of Sophia, Franc didn't find a husband or another career path while away at college. She did, however, have a lot of fun and meet a lot of nice guys. She even dated a few, but not one of them was special enough to keep her from coming home to her roots at *Franc's*. So shortly after graduation with her degree in hand, she returned home to learn the family business once again. Over the next seventeen years, Franc worked alongside her dad. It was the most amazing experience of her life. They started each day with a cup of coffee while looking over the last night's numbers, and they finished each night with a glass of Syrah while planning the schedule and menu for the next day. Her dad taught Franc not only how to run the business but also how to encourage the best from their employees. She noted that even when things got heated, her dad always made sure everyone involved could resolve the disagreement with mutual respect and dignity.

Both of Franc's parents took great pride in how they treated their customers. When patrons called to make their reservations for upcoming nights, her mother made sure to ask if they were celebrating anything special that evening before hanging up the phone. She felt it was very important to make each person who walked through the doors of *Franc's* feel as if he or she were visiting an old family member's home. She made careful notes of each special reservation and then asked the kitchen to make the appropriate dessert, meal, or drink. For instance, if a party called in to reserve a table for someone's birthday, she always made sure there was a special dessert made ahead of time to be presented at the end of the meal as a gift from the restaurant. Other times she would have complimentary bottles of champagne delivered to the tables celebrating anniversaries or engagements. These were her ways of thanking the customers for including *Franc's* as a part of their celebration of the milestones in their lives. Franc's dad also made sure to leave the kitchen throughout the night and walk through the dining room, introducing himself to each of the tables and sincerely thanking the patrons for coming in that night. Through the years Franc watched as some of these patrons became more than customers; they became an extension of her own family. They watched as children grew up, graduated, married, and later brought their own families into *Franc's* to celebrate some of their own milestones.

The years working alongside her dad changed their relationship from mentor and student to colleague and friend. It was a time in her life she will treasure forever. Tragically, the day before Franc's forty-first birthday, her father died of an aneurysm while on his way to work. She remembers the exact moment she got the phone call from her older sister, Maria, giving her the devastating news. She was standing in the kitchen still in her bathrobe as Maria's words came through the receiver and filled the room. Within an instant Franc felt her legs give way and her body drop to the hard stone floor in a lifeless heap. She sat bare legged against the cold stone with tears streaming down her face and onto her robe. She also remembers feeling as if time stood still, the world no longer spinning and the room suddenly becoming void of air. As she gasped to catch her breath, shocked and confused, she began to question her sister. "What? How? When?" Then with great concern, she added, "Oh God! How's Mom?"

In the days that followed, not only did the restaurant become Franc's responsibility, but it also became her sanctuary, her focus, and her comfort. Sitting at her father's desk, she could still smell the fragrance of his Old

Spice aftershave floating in the air. The picture of her and her sisters from a family vacation to Niagara Falls still sits on the corner of his desk, next to a photo of her parents from their fiftieth wedding anniversary celebration here at the restaurant. Their anniversary party was a beautiful, huge private party on a hot mid-August night. The restaurant was filled with family and friends eating, drinking, and laughing. Her father's brother, Joe, and his band played songs of the Rat Pack era while Franc's parents danced all evening. She remembers thinking how beautiful her mom looked in her lavender dress. It was fitted at the waist and gave way to a full knee-length skirt. So every time Franc's dad swung her around on the dance floor, her skirt opened like flower petals swaying in the breeze. Seeing the two of them so happy and completely in love is one of Franc's favorite memories.

On the wall to the right of Franc's desk, hanging just above the calendar, is a photo taken in the early seventies of her dad and grandfather standing under the awning of their restaurant. Each day before Franc opens the doors of the restaurant to customers, she takes a few minutes to look at the photo to remember the legacy that has come before her and to do her best each day to honor the family name.

CHAPTER 2

TEN YEARS EARLIER: BOOK CLUB IS BORN

Melissa and her husband, Ryan, arrive at the Marcus Hotel, a five-star hotel on East Fifty-Seventh Street in Midtown Manhattan. The hotel is one of the city's oldest and most famous landmarks. Tonight is a dark and chilly November evening, which makes the warm glow from the hotel lobby even more inviting than usual. The Marcus Hotel was built in the early 1900s and still boasts all of its prewar glory. Every detail in the hotel is a work of art, from its high coffered ceilings to its plaster moldings, ebony hardwood floors with marble walkways to its columns and gilded corbels, making each room feel more lavish than the last. The massive granite fireplace in the grand lobby and oversize wingback chairs beckon travelers to sip on cocktails and relax the night away. The Marcus stands as a testament to the beauty of the era, when people took great pride in their work, craftsmanship, and artistry. It has the type of skill and craftsmanship that can't be matched today because of the limitations, deadlines, and cost-cutting mind-set of most modern-day builders and financiers.

Before exiting their car, Melissa checks her lipstick and hair in the visor mirror one last time. Looking through her silver-beaded clutch, she finds just the right shade of soft pink lipstick for a quick application then fluffs her pageant-ready blond locks. Noticing his wife looks nervous, Ryan turns toward Melissa and, with a smile on his face, assures her that she looks great. Exiting the car now, Ryan gives his black Volvo SUV keys to the waiting valet and walks around to the other side of the car to take Melissa's hand. As they continue toward the entrance, they both pause to gaze at the sheer beauty of the grand hotel, remembering that this was Ryan's inspiration for the design he created for the new cancer wing being honored at tonight's gala. While in the lobby, Ryan proudly notices the poster-size images of the new wing on display. The renderings set amid the backdrop of the grand hotel make him smile with confidence of a job well done. The lobby is bustling with some of the city's most wealthy and influential people, all dressed in their finest black-tie attire. Before entering to the large banquet hall, they stop to check their coats with the three attendants standing behind a large table. After waiting patiently in line, they take their turns handing their coats to a young woman dressed in a modest black dress with her dark hair pulled tightly in a low bun. Taking her coat off and handing it to the clerk, Melissa reveals her outfit. It is an electric-blue, floor-length gown with sequins at the bust, which stands out in a sea of black. The dress is tasteful but somehow reminiscent of a prom dress, not quite the right choice for an evening gala or, for that matter, someone in her midthirties. As the attendant takes Melissa's coat, she can't help but chuckle softly to herself. She then kindly hands Melissa her coat ticket, along with a smile and a nod, as she thanks her for coming and wishes her and her husband a wonderful time at tonight's event. Melissa is relieved by the smile and is convinced from the nod that she must look amazing in her new gown. With her new boost of self-assurance, she takes Ryan's arm and confidently enters the hall.

As they embark into the room, Melissa is overcome with the beauty of it all. The warmth of the crystal chandeliers, the opulence of the marble walkways, the gold-gilded moldings, and the red floral carpet have transported Melissa in her thoughts to a time long ago. She imagines what it must have been like to attend a ball here when the hotel was first built. "Spectacular," she whispers quietly. The hall is already teeming with ladies in designer gowns draped in jewelry and men looking dapper in their tuxedos. "What a wonderful night," she adds softly.

Prominently displayed on easels in the center of the room are more renderings and a model of the hospital's new cancer wing. "The drawings of the new wing look beautiful, Ryan. You did an amazing job." Ryan smiles with gratitude; he knows how lucky he is to have such a wonderful and supportive wife.

They met their junior year at Western Washington University, located in the northwest corner of Washington State, and have been together ever since. Western Washington University is housed in one of those progressive university towns, right on the banks of the Puget Sound and tucked away neatly behind the San Juan Islands. The always-green, temperate climate of Bellingham, Washington, made the sunny days on campus warm and inviting. Melissa likes to tell people of the time she saw Ryan, a handsome young man with dark, wavy hair, sitting around the fountain in Red Square and how she choreographed their meeting. She tells of how she mustered up the courage to walk over and sit next to him on the brick-lined ledge surrounding the fountain. Trying to get his attention, she precariously set her book bag down in a way that allowed her textbook to fall out. Ryan, being the gentleman he is, bent over, picked up the book, and handed it back to her. Then, as he gave the book back to her, he introduced himself, and they have been together ever since.

To this day Ryan still lets Melissa believe that she orchestrated their meeting, when in fact it was Ryan all along. The truth is, weeks before their infamous meeting at the fountain, Ryan had spotted Melissa one afternoon while looking out onto the square from the engineering building, daydreaming. He thought she was the most beautiful girl he had ever seen. So he spent the next few weeks sitting in the same spot at the fountain, in hopes she would come by. He had always meant to tell her the truth about their meeting, but after listening to Melissa say how proud she was of herself for having the boldness to approach him, Ryan decided to keep quiet.

Melissa also notices how each of the tables in the hall are draped to the floor in plum-colored cloth to represent cancer caregivers and topped with a gorgeous floral arrangement in a rainbow of colors. Each floral arrangement is different to symbolize the many kinds of cancer: pink flowers for breast cancer, orange flowers for kidney cancer, rose-dyed teal for cervical cancer, and so on.

Walking around the room, they look to see who they might know. Glancing toward the bar, Ryan spots a colleague of his named Sarah. She is a beautiful thirty-something brunette dressed in a chic winter-white off-the-shoulder short dress. Sarah is standing alone, with a glass of white wine in her hand, trying hard to look as if she is having a nice time. Ryan points her out to Melissa and then takes her over to meet Sarah.

Melissa immediately notices Sarah's gorgeous shoes. They are platinum pumps with crystal details on the back. Impressed with Sarah's fashion sense, Melissa gives her a mental nod of approval. Ryan does the introductions and tells Melissa that Sarah is the one who did the community campaign and slogan for the hospital's new wing.

"So that was you who came up with '*Hope*, the four-letter word that's okay to shout!' I think it's brilliant," Melissa says with a smile.

Flattered by Melissa's compliment, Sarah modestly looks down, smiles, and gestures a royal curtsy while saying, "Well, thank you."

The next few moments are spent with polite small talk. Feeling a little out of place attending the gala alone, and not really knowing many of the other faces in the room, Sarah is grateful to have someone to talk with. However, she keeps finding herself feeling distracted while Melissa tells stories about the vacation she and Ryan took to Mexico last summer. She can't stop herself from staring, first at Melissa's outfit and then upward to her bouffant. She is trying to decide if it's the big blond hair or the vibrant blue gown that is giving her the idea that Melissa looks like Barbie. And yet, Sarah has to concede that whatever it is, somehow it totally works for her. It doesn't take her long to recognize that this big blond Barbie, with her engaging smile and never-ending stories, and she are going to become great friends.

Noticing Sarah's attention to her outfit, Melissa takes the interest as a sure sign that Sarah has impeccable taste. Ignoring Ryan completely as they make their way to the renderings and model of the new wing, the two kindred spirits spend the next few minutes scanning the room and commenting on each of the guests' outfits—some good, some bad, and some "Seriously, what was she thinking?"

Approaching the table with the reproduction, Sarah comments, "It is just so beautiful. I know I've seen it a hundred times before while I was working on the campaign, but it never fails to hold my attention." As she gently runs her elegant fingers across the building and along the stand of small trees and landscape lining the entrance of the building, she can't help but be reminded of the model train she had as a child. The train, which was lovingly referred to as "Trapper," was a gift her dad had received as a child that later was passed down to Sarah. She has so many cherished memories of sitting around their fifteen-foot, sparkling Christmas tree, watching in awe as her dad steered the small coal train around the track. Sarah paid close attention to how gingerly he maneuvered the levers enabling Trapper to sail through the windy course constructed under the giant glowing tree. When it was Sarah's turn to man the operator's panel, she made sure to be ever so careful to slow the train down just enough so it would stay on the track while curving through the small Bavarian village, but not so slow as to cause Trapper to stop. She controlled the small train just as she had watched her dad do successfully so many times before. It took patience, concentration, attention to detail, and a steady hand to make a complete rotation around the track, something her two older brothers had not quite developed. It was this meticulous attention to detail that would later be both a blessing and an obstacle for Sarah in so many ways. One Christmas Eve at the young age of seven, the monumental job of conductor was ceremoniously granted to Sarah by her father. She will never forget the feeling of accomplishment and the look on her dad's face as he placed the striped blue-and-white cap upon her head and called her "Conductor," a nickname that would stick with her forever.

A few minutes later, Ryan notices an older gentleman sporting a comb-over rivaling Donald Trump's and his elegant wife walking into the banquet hall. Leaning down toward Melissa's ear, Ryan quietly says that he needs to go talk to Mr. Anderson. Melissa looks over toward the entrance to see which couple he is talking about and waves Ryan away without hesitation. "Oh, I'm good. Why don't you just go on over? I'll stay here with Sarah." Knowing the way his wife feels about Mr. Anderson, Ryan excuses himself and says he won't be gone long.

Sarah, thinking Melissa stayed behind because she feels sorry for her attending the gala alone, tells Melissa, "It's really okay. You don't have to stay here with me."

"Are you kidding? You're the one doing me a favor." Melissa continues while looking over her shoulder toward Ryan and Mr. Anderson, saying, "That guy's an ass. He has been stringing Ryan along for months, telling him that he's one of the guys in the running for a new high-rise he's putting up on the Upper East Side. Who knows when he'll make his decision. I think he just likes the attention he gets from potential architects vying for the job. Not to mention Ryan says he's a complete letch. He told me that when they go to lunch to discuss upcoming projects, Mr. Anderson likes to get grabby with the waitresses and make inappropriate comments to them."

Angered by the news, Sarah looks over at Ryan and Mr. Anderson and gives the old perv a look of disgust while shaking her head. "Jerk."

Melissa says patronizingly, "And look at his wife, standing there in last year's fashion with that innocent smile on her face. Poor thing, she has no idea who she's really married to."

Just as she finishes her sentence, a woman in her mid-fifties dressed in a black pantsuit approaches the vacant podium on the stage and announces that it is time for everyone to take their seats for dinner, which will then be followed by the award ceremony. Sarah is thankful that before the dinner announcement had been made she and Melissa, in covert moves, changed place cards with another table so Sarah could sit with them instead of sitting alone at a table where she didn't know anyone.

Ryan walks back to join them as they are about to take their seats.

After dinner, drinks, and many conversations from current events to stories of their childhoods, Sarah reveals to Melissa why she is at the gala alone tonight, confiding that she and her boyfriend of seven years have recently broken up. And to make matters worse, she adds that she is now on the hunt to find a new apartment because her current lease is too expensive for her to afford on her own. Melissa, not one to shy away from a juicy story, immediately asks Sarah why they broke up.

"Well, let's see…it might have to do with the fact that I came home from work last week in the middle of the afternoon because I wasn't feeling well to find Sam in bed with the neighbor from down the hall."

Intrigued, Melissa whispers, "Was it a guy?"

"What?" Sarah says, shaking her head, confused and surprised by the question. "No, it wasn't a guy. It was a lady. And I use the term *lady* generously."

"Well, I had to ask," said Melissa innocently.

Sarah explains to her that she kicked Sam out, and that's why she needs a smaller place. Happy to be of some help, Melissa tells Sarah about her good friend Rita. "I know a great broker. Her name is Rita. You will love her. Her twin boys and my daughter, Rachael, have been going to the same school since kindergarten. We've been on dozens of PTA committees together. She and her husband, Jim, just opened their own real-estate company." She goes on to tell Sarah all about Rita and Jim. "That's how they met. They were both agents at the same brokerage. I am not sure how she does it. I mean, I love spending time with Ryan, but I'm not sure I could handle every moment of my day with him," she says, raising her eyebrow. "Anyway, I'll introduce you to her. I am sure they're here tonight." Melissa looks around the room. "Jim's dad died of brain cancer three years ago. It was really devastating to the whole family. Since then they've been heavily involved in fund-raising for cancer awareness."

At another table at the gala sits Kathy, a middle-aged, round woman dressed in a tailored navy suit with white piping on the lapel, flanked by two thunderous men. On the one side of Kathy sits a young, flashy, arrogant local politician and on the other a middle-aged man, with a beer belly and thinning hair, who happens to be a member of the hospital board. It is obvious by the rolling of her eyes that Kathy is annoyed by the conversation the men are having across the front of her as if she's not there and is having a tough time keeping quiet. Which has her thinking to herself, "This guy is just full of crap," and questioning, "Who were the morons that voted for him?" Listening to the two drone on about the clichés of welfare, campaign funding, and reelections, Kathy wishes her husband could have come with her tonight instead of being away on a business trip. At least then, no matter how boring or ignorant the conversation got at the table, she would have had him to keep her company. He would also be there to remind her that as a nurse in the hospital, she can't just let herself go off on these pompous blowhards, especially not the hospital board member. However, that doesn't stop her from fantasizing about telling these privileged idiots what she really thinks of them and their narrow-minded views or how she would like to educate them on what it is really like to be faced with the realities of poverty.

Kathy is all too familiar with the challenges of living on lower incomes. She grew up with a loving family in a small town in Pennsylvania. Her parents did their best, but despite their efforts, without a formal education, it was tough to make ends meet at the end of each month. Kathy was one of four girls, where reduced school-lunch tickets and hand-me-down clothes were a way of life. Unfortunately for Kathy, being the youngest meant that by the time the clothes got to her, most of them were threadbare and stained. This was something that the other girls at school had been all too happy to point out to anyone who would listen. Like the time when Kathy was in the second grade and she and her classmates were lining up to go outside. Finding her place in line, Kathy smiled joyfully when she saw Becky Sanders standing behind her, thinking maybe today would be the day that Becky asked her to join her and the other girls in a game of chase with the boys. Becky was the most popular girl in school, and

Kathy envied her. The way Becky looked and dressed was something Kathy could only dream about. She wore beautiful dresses, with matching cardigans, and colorful bows in her long, wavy blond hair, but best of all, Becky wore the most beautiful, shiniest black-and-white saddle Mary Janes that Kathy had ever seen. This while Kathy was stuck wearing her older sister Susan's scuffed hand-me-down shoes that now sported a small hole near the big-toe area on the right shoe, which let water seep in when Kathy splashed through the puddles on her way home from school. As their teacher, Mrs. Trimmer, was busy in the back of the classroom gathering the jump ropes and rubber balls for the playground, Kathy's hopes of inclusion vanished when Becky leaned forward and spit on her shoes. Pointing and laughing loudly to the other kids, she innocently explained that she was just trying to improve the way they looked by making them shine.

When you are a child, you want nothing more than to fit in. Unfortunately, more often than not, the "Beckys" of this world seem to let the "Kathys" of this world know that they are different, convincing them that somehow, just because they don't have the latest clothes, live in the fanciest homes, or belong to the country club, they are somehow less worthy. Despite the constant bullying and teasing, the one thing that Kathy knew she had that was more precious than all of Becky's fancy dresses and shiny shoes were parents that loved her unconditionally and sisters that would stand by her through thick and thin. She had a real family, the always-on-your-side, going-to-have-your-back-no-matter-what kind of family. Through the best of times and the worst, her family would always be the constant rock in Kathy's life.

This truth was never more evident than when Kathy was ten and her mother was diagnosed with uterine cancer. That was when her grandma Gwyn moved into their home and never moved out. Kathy remembers when her parents sat her and her sisters down to tell them the news. She and her sisters had spent the last two weeks going to their next-door neighbor Ms. O'Donnell's house every day after school instead of going home. It was a cold, cloudy evening in October when Ms. O'Donnell got a phone call from Kathy's dad. He told her that Kathy's mom and he were home from their appointment and it was time for the girls to come home. When Kathy and her sisters walked through the doorway of their home, they could see the evidence on both their parents' faces that they had been crying.

As Kathy took a seat next to her mom on the plaid sofa, her dad started to explain why their mom had been so tired for the past few months. The next day Kathy and one of her sisters moved out of the room that they had shared and into their older sisters' room down the hall. Later that same day, her grandmother moved in, and within eleven months Kathy's mom had passed away. Kathy remembers feeling, even as a child, that if they hadn't been so poor, her mother could have gone to the doctor sooner, and maybe then she would have had a fighting chance to beat her cancer. Not only had the cancer taken her mother, but it also robbed her of her innocence of youth. Rather than let this tragedy break her, Kathy used her anger and grief to drive her to do well in school and later pursue a career in the medical field. Kathy knows that it was through her difficult childhood that she found strength and compassion, the very qualities that make her a great nurse and leader today.

Fed up with the discussion at her table, Kathy abruptly excuses herself and makes her way to the bathroom, any excuse to get away from these jackasses. As she enters the bathroom, she passes through the ladies' lounge area on her way to the washroom. The lounge is furnished with two burgundy velour settees and three gilded vanities stocked with small antique perfume bottles and tins of mints. Through the next set of doors, she enters the washroom and walks over to the long marble counter that holds four brass sinks to wash her hands and splash water on her face, in an attempt to cool her temper. While running the water, she can't help but mumble about the idiots at her table, mocking and repeating their ignorant views to herself in the mirror...

"People on welfare are lazy."

"If we keep giving them handouts, they will never find jobs."

"All they do is sit on the sofa all day, drinking beer and smoking their cigarettes, waiting for the mailman to bring them their paycheck."

"What the hell does he know about welfare? I bet the only thing that city councilman had to worry about when he was a child was where they would travel for Christmas break...Aspen or Whistler," Kathy says sarcastically.

Hearing a snicker from one of the stalls, Kathy quickly turns around to see a very striking woman about her age emerging from the door. She is wearing a black A-line skirt, zebra-print pumps, and a crisp, tailored white blouse accessorized by a chunky necklace of layers of gold chains and pearls.

"Oh, don't worry about Councilman Ward," the woman says. "He's an arrogant prick. His family probably bought him the election. That kind of stupidity can only be hidden once. I'm sure by now everyone sees through his perfect teeth and spray-on tan to the racist elitist that he really is," comments the woman as she washes her hands.

Impressed by the woman's snarky quip, Kathy immediately introduces herself. "Hi, I'm Kathy. I'm an ER nurse at the hospital."

Extending her hand, the quick-witted woman responds, "I'm Diane. I own a florist shop on the Upper East Side, Petals. We donated the flowers for tonight's event." She explains to Kathy that a dear friend of hers died this past year from prostate cancer, and it was her way of saying thank you to the wonderful staff of doctors, nurses, and specialists who took care of him.

Continuing to make small talk as they walk out of the bathroom and head down the hall leading back to the banquet room, Diane notices Kathy pausing at the doorway and taking a few deep breaths before she heads back to her table.

Looking toward the table, they can both see the councilman laughing robustly with the board member at the table. Kathy looks to Diane and with a sarcastic tone says, "He's probably telling a joke about dwarfs having sex with horses," which brings Diane to burst out in laughter. Not bearing the idea of going back to her table, Kathy then asks Diane if she'd like to go to the bar.

Glancing toward the councilman, Diane eagerly replies, "Good idea."

At the bar Kathy and Diane continue to visit while listening to the ceremony. They are both thrilled to hear how much money has been raised to help with the cost of the new cancer wing. Once all the announcements have been made, speakers have taken their turns at the podium, and awards have been handed out, the guests are now encouraged to begin moving around the banquet hall to mingle with one another.

Across the room, at a table near the stage, Bette Thompson spots her old friend Diane talking with a woman at the bar. Bette is a vibrant, self-confident woman in her early fifties. She has tussled, carefree, shoulder-length, strawberry-blond hair and is dressed to-night in one of her signature vintage floral caftans from the seventies. She is accompanied tonight by a young, gorgeous blonde named Ali. Ali, who looks like the complete contrast to Bette, is dressed in a simple red sheath that was left over from her sorority days at UCLA. Happy to see Diane at the event tonight, Bette walks over to say hello and introduce her to her new friend Ali.

Ali is a new morning-news host for the show *Good Morning New York*. She moved from California four months ago and is still trying to find her bearings around the studio and the city. The morning of the gala, Ali arrived to the TV studio just before five for the morning meeting and was thrilled to see that there were once again doughnuts and coffee in the conference room. While enjoying her second cup of coffee and third doughnut, she noticed that across the table from her, Candice Edwards, a senior newswoman who had been with *Good Morning New York* for the past fifteen years, was glaring at her. Ali couldn't imagine why Candice would be angry with her. She had hardly had a conversation with her since she began working for the station. "What could I have done to offend her?" Then, without warning, the show's producer, Stanley, interrupted Ali's train of thought by announcing to everyone in the room that he would like to appoint Ali to cover the White House during this year's presidential election. He explained that some of the sponsors and other executives were hoping that Ali would be able to bring in a younger audience. They were hoping to change their image on how they report on politics to include the younger generation, similar to what MTV was doing.

Ali just about choked on her bite of powdered-sugar doughnut when she heard Stanley's shocking declaration. She couldn't believe what she was hearing, barely thirty and being given such a large assignment. As the meeting came to an end, Ali walked out of the boardroom and hurried down the hall to walk alongside Candice. "Wow, I can't believe that just happened. I mean, Stanley wants me to cover the election. I had no idea that was going to happen. I thought for sure you would be doing it again. You've been doing it for as long as I can remember." Ali went on to say, "I had nothing to do with it. I hope you aren't mad at me."

Annoyed with Ali's rambling, Candice abruptly stopped walking, sharply turned toward her, and judgmentally looked her up and down, never saying a word. She then silently turned and walked away knowing full well that she had been replaced by youth and beauty.

Later that same day, Ali interviewed Bette Thompson for a segment on *Good Morning New York*. Bette had written many single-ladies guides, and now her new book, *Living for You in a City of Millions*, was on the *New York Times* best-seller list. During the interview, Ali told Bette how much she loved the book, saying that she was given a copy of Bette's book as a going-away gift from her co-workers at her last job before moving to New York.

Bette had been on the show many times before, but this was the first time she was interviewed by Ali, and she hadn't been quite sure what to expect from such a young newbie to the show. However, to Bette's delight, the interview went marvelously; it was like talking with an old friend. It turned out they both graduated from the same university, albeit Bette did it nineteen years prior, and it was fun for Bette to hear they actually had some of the same professors.

During one of the commercial breaks, Ali confessed to Bette that she kept the book with her at all times. In fact, it was in her bag in her dressing room right then, and she had read it from cover to cover so many times that she could probably quote most of it back to Bette. She added that being new to the city and not having made many friends yet, the book had played an integral role in making her feel more self-assured and confident while getting around and exploring the city by herself.

Visiting with Ali during these breaks, Bette found herself intrigued by Ali's youth and excitement for her new career. She remembered what it was like as a young woman herself, just starting out as a journalist for the *New York Times*, a field that had previously been domi-nated by men, before branching out on her own as an author. Realizing she saw a little of herself in Ali, she felt an instant connection. So after the interview was over and as the crew began mingling around the set getting things ready for the next segment, Bette surprised Ali by asking if she would like to go with her tonight to a fund-raising gala for a new cancer wing being held at the Marcus Hotel. She explained to Ali that the event tonight was very near and dear to her heart because a close friend of hers had passed away from prostate cancer last year. Before giving Ali a chance to answer, Bette persuasively said, "Come on. Say yes. There are going to be many people there you should meet, and besides, it's a chance to get dressed up and go out on the town. What do you say?" She also told Ali that one of her closest friends, Diane, would be there tonight. "She owns a floral shop downtown and did all the arrangements for tonight. It's going to be beautiful." She added, "And Diane is definitely someone you should know." She explained that Diane does all the flowers for the big events in Manhattan and knows all the gossip about who's doing what and with whom they are doing it. Overjoyed by the invitation, Ali accepted without hesitation.

On the other side of the banquet hall, Rita and Jim get up from their table and start to mingle around the room. They are quite the striking couple: both tall, fit, and well dressed. Rita's long, wavy dark hair complements her tailored, short, sequined, black backless dress flawlessly. The cut and fit of the dress allow Rita to show off her toned back in a tasteful yet provocative way. Jim looks dapper in his slim-fitted black tuxedo with his premature salt-and-pepper hair. And together, they look absolutely stunning standing next to one another.

While they are visiting with a small group of fundraisers, the conversation goes from raising money for cancer research to baseball. Instantly Rita is bored by the change of subject, because in her opinion there is only one sport worth watching or caring about, and that is, of course, football. Like her daddy always preached, "Watching anything else is a waste of time." Glancing around the room looking for a polite exit plan, Rita notices a familiar face talking with a group of ladies at the bar. It's Kathy, the ER nurse who took care of their son John after he hurt his leg in last week's soccer game. Happy to have a reason to walk away from such a "riveting" conversation, she tells her husband that she is going over to thank the ER nurse for the wonderful care she gave their son. Smiling politely to the others as they continue recapping the Yankees' last season stats, Rita quietly excuses herself before quickly making her escape to the bar and Kathy.

A few moments later, Melissa, Ryan, and Sarah bump into Jim while on their way to look at the memorial photos of current and past cancer patients being displayed on the "Table of Honor." Happily, Melissa smiles and says to Jim, "Hi, glad we ran into you. Is Rita here with you? I was going to introduce her to Sarah." She explains, "She is looking for a new place to rent, and I was thinking Rita could help her with the hunt."

After introductions, Jim says to Sarah, "A new place, that's great. Rita can totally help you with that. She handles the residential side, while I try to focus more on the commercial side of things."

Looking back to Melissa now, Jim tells her, "Rita is over by the bar, talking to the ER nurse who took care of John last week. We had to bring him in after he hurt his leg at the soccer game."

"Oh yeah, I heard about that. Ouch, poor little guy. How's he doing?"

"The doctor says he'll be fine in a few weeks. It was just a bad sprain. And besides, I think he likes all the attention he's getting from the other kids at school. Although, I don't think his brother likes the idea of carrying John's backpack to and from class each day."

As Melissa and Sarah start to walk away, Jim adds, "It was nice to meet you, Sarah. Good luck with the house hunt."

Sarah smiles and says, "It was nice to meet you too, and thanks. I hope I can find something soon."

Melissa leads Sarah across the room to introduce her to Rita. After cordial introductions, she bluntly explains to Rita that Sarah is looking for a new apartment because one afternoon she came home to find her boyfriend of seven years in bed with their neighbor.

"What? Are you kidding me? That's awful," exclaims Rita.

Sarah, mortified by this loud outburst, doesn't answer. Instead she sheepishly nods and gives a half smile.

Standing so close to Rita, the foursome of Kathy, Diane, Bette, and Ali can't help but overhear the conversation and turn to look at Sarah with sympathy. Instinctually, the ladies gather around Sarah to give her their support and to agree what jerks some men can be, sharing their own stories of love and heartbreak. Before long, Bette notices an empty table and suggests they all go over and take a seat where they can continue the conversation more comfortably. Just as they sit down, Kathy sees a waiter walking by the table and grabs his arm. Stopping him in his tracks, she informs him, "We are going to need a few bottles of wine brought to the table."

The waiter pauses to take a look at the ladies sitting around the table. It is clear from the expressions on the faces peering back at him that something big just happened and more than likely has to do with a man. Not daring to ask questions, he nods submissively and leaves to retrieve the wine. He returns a few minutes later with four bottles of wine, two white and two red, along with glasses for each of the ladies. The women continue to sit together, drinking, talking, and eventually laughing for the remainder of the evening. Ali advises Sarah to get a good book to keep her company at night. She explains that, as a single woman, that's what she does. Speaking from experience, she says, "You need something funny to lift your spirits. And there is nothing better than a good laugh-out-loud kind of book."

"Maybe something about a woman who gets back at her cheating husband by writing 'Impotent' across his forehead with permanent marker while he's asleep," says Diane, laughing.

Hearing this unexpected suggestion from her new-found friend, Sarah just about spits out her wine. After catching her breath, she replies, "Now, that sounds like a book I would read!"

"Well," says Bette sarcastically, "I am a writer; just give me a little time. I'm sure I could come up with something."

Bette's comment is met with laughter and a resounding "I'd read that!"

Melissa tells the group that she just finished a funny book; it's not about getting even with an ex, but it is funny. It is about a woman and the culture shock she has while traveling through Japan. Rita chimes in and says she read that book too, and it is really funny. Kathy adds that she heard about that book from one of her coworkers and has been meaning to read it.

"It does sound interesting. Maybe I'll stop by and pick up a copy on my way home tonight. Anything to help with the long nights," admits Sarah.

"I'd love to hear what you think of the book after you finish. I hope you find it as funny as I did. I mean, some of the things that poor lady went through. I don't want to spoil it, but, seriously, it is so funny!" replies Melissa.

"I can always use a good laugh. Think I'll give it a try too," says Diane.

When the waiter stops by the table to ask if he can get them anything else, they are suddenly aware that most of the guests have already gone for the evening. Rita and Melissa can see that Jim and Ryan are visiting with each other by the renderings but are clearly ready to leave. The ladies have been having such a good time that none of them noticed how long they had been sitting together or how late it had gotten. Sad to see the evening come to an end, they decide to set a date to meet together one evening in the coming weeks over a good meal and drinks to discuss the book. They settle on an Italian restaurant named *Franc's*. It's conveniently located and has been recently praised in the *New York Times* as one of the city's top restaurants for authentic Italian cuisine. So, as the evening comes to a close, phone numbers are exchanged, friendships are made, and book club is born.

CHAPTER 3

PRESENT DAY: GETTING READY FOR BOOK CLUB

Bette Preparing Dinner Two Hours before Book Club

Bette stands in the kitchen of her eighteenth-floor eclectic apartment, happily humming along to an old Barbra Streisand song playing on her iPhone, which is docked on the counter. She is decked out in her new, crisp blue-and-white-striped apron, which still has its tags left on from Pottery Barn. Despite being new, her apron is already covered in smears and splatters, even though Bette's cooking debut has just begun. On the white marble countertop sits the Barefoot Contessa, Ina Garten's, cookbook *Foolproof*, which Bette picked up from the corner bookstore on her way home from a lunch meeting she had last week with her editor. The book is open and dog-eared to a recipe on page 118, "Chicken with Wild Mushrooms." With sweat beading on her forehead, she carefully follows each step laid out in the recipe as if she were defusing a bomb.

Thirty minutes later, the chicken is now out of the oven, and Bette begins to remove each piece from the pot. Placing the pieces on an oval platter next to the stove, Bette takes a moment to admire her culinary work of art. "I can't believe I made this. The chicken actually looks good," she praises to herself.

Checking the recipe every few moments to make sure she is following it correctly, Bette begins mashing butter and flour together in a small bowl and then adds it to the pot that is still bubbling with the remaining juices left behind by the chicken. She questions Ina *and* her cookbook. "Are you sure? This doesn't look anything like gravy." Staying the course, she stirs constantly over medium heat for five minutes. To her delight, what looked like a mess is actually coming together to create a beautiful brown sauce. Taking a spoon from the drawer, Bette hesitates before dipping it into the pot and tasting the bubbling concoction. She is surprised and overjoyed to find it tastes delicious. With a smile on her face, she leans over the cookbook and states, "Ina Garten, my friend, you were right. It is foolproof."

Continuing to follow the recipe, she places the chicken back into the pot and turns the stove off. With excitement in her voice, she praises her accomplishment. "I can't believe I did it. I made a home-cooked meal for my loving husband. Harry is going to be so impressed!" Although Bette has won many awards and received countless accolades for her written work, such as her best-selling books *Table for One* and *A Single's Guide to the Universe*, this is, by far, one of the most rewarding things she has ever done. Looking at the time on the clock that hangs above the bistro table tucked in the corner of the small kitchen, Bette knows it is time for her to take off her apron and get cleaned up for her night out with her girlfriends.

As she stands in front of the mirror above the vanity in the bathroom, she can't help but raise her left hand to see the image of her beautiful wedding ring reflecting back at her. She has never been so happy.

Freshly showered and dressed, she is ready for tonight's gathering. Stopping by the kitchen, Bette checks to make sure the chicken with wild mushrooms has cooled down enough to be placed in the refrigerator. After doing so, she goes to her home office and pulls out a pad of paper from the center drawer of her desk. On the paper, she scribes a note encased with a large red heart to leave on the counter for her husband to see when he gets home from work later that evening. It reads, "Darling, dinner is in the fridge. Enjoy! See you tonight," followed by a winky face. Next she draws another heart in red on a different sheet of paper; this one she tapes to the lid of the pot holding her delicious masterpiece in the refrigerator. Finally, she makes her way to the foyer, where she puts on her gloves, grabs her book nested on the entry console table, and leaves to catch the waiting cab to take her to *Franc's*.

⊨ ⊨

Melissa Driving to Book Club

Melissa and Ryan are in their car, headed down Third Avenue, making their way to *Franc's*. Ryan is dropping Melissa off at the restaurant on his way to the gym. He and Rita's husband, Jim, along with two other guys, meet up every other Thursday at the gym on Boyer Street to play racquetball and catch up. Ryan jokingly refers to it as a guys' version of book club.

At a stoplight just two blocks from the restaurant, Melissa notices Ryan looking in her direction with a wide, goofy grin on his face. "What is that big smile for?" she asks.

"I can't believe you kept the napkin with the drawing of La Nourriture all this time. And you showed it to Rachael."

With a smile on her face, Melissa reaches over, takes hold of Ryan's hand, and softly says to him, "Of course I kept it. It means the world to me."

When they pull up in front of *Franc's*, Melissa leans over and kisses Ryan good-bye. She wishes him good luck at the gym, adding that she hopes he and Jim crush the other guys on the court tonight. She also reminds him that she is going to share a cab home with Rita after book club.

As Melissa shuts the car door behind her and starts to walk away, she begins adjusting her top and fidgeting with her hair, making sure everything looks just so. Checking over his shoulder for traffic, Ryan notices Melissa's book is still sitting on the backseat. He immediately unrolls the window and shouts Melissa's name while holding the book up for her to see. When she returns to the car to retrieve her book, Ryan offers the book, but not before he tells her how beautiful she looks tonight. Blushing, she takes her book and starts to walk away from the car, but this time she walks with an exaggerated sway in her step and a smile on her face, knowing he is watching her. Confident with the thought of this, she doesn't dare look back.

***

Sarah Leaving Her Office and Heading Out to Book Club

Pacing back and forth from one end of her executive office to the other, Sarah is struggling to find the words for a new product. Her deadline to come up with a new ad campaign is only a week away. However, she knows at tomorrow's staff meeting she is supposed to give the team her finalized storyboard and show them her ad pitch. It's the same one she will be presenting to the clients the following week. Sarah has struggled to find just the right words for different products in the past, but has always found that moment of clarity when, for whatever reason, fate steps in and the words just appear. Sometimes she finds inspiration in the most random places. One time she came up with a jingle for a new toothpaste while watching the ballet; something about the perfectly timed movements and the white feathers in the dancers' hair reminded her of a tooth's enamel. Another time she was riding the subway and noticed a fellow passenger was wearing a pair of rain boots adorned with bright-pink elephants, which in turn inspired her slogan for a new residential construction company: "For a home they'll never forget."

Unfortunately, she has not been so lucky this time. Each idea she says aloud to herself sounds more ridiculous than the previous. Even after using the product, she still cannot come up with a solid pitch. Hoping for inspiration, she stops to look out the floor-to-ceiling window of her office space. From her window, she can see crowds of pedestrians walking up and down the street. She notices how they move in what looks like a choreographed motion so as not to run into one another. They remind her of when she was a little girl. On Sunday evenings after her bath, Sarah's mom would turn on *Mutual of Omaha's Wild Kingdom*. Sarah, her younger sister, and her two older brothers would sit with their fresh, damp hair and warm pajamas, snuggled together under blankets on the sofa. There they would sit, glued to the television, intrigued and excited for what tonight's episode might bring; alligators, gorillas, sea life, they were all amazing. The scene out her window today reminded her of one of the episodes showing ants navigating the jungle floor, each ant moving on its own path toward a specific job and destination only known to it.

With Sarah's thoughts drifting to her childhood, she is startled when her secretary, a young red-headed woman in her early twenties, enters her office. "Excuse me, Sarah. It's six thirty. You asked me to remind you that you have book club tonight," says Mary, interrupting Sarah's gaze out the window.

Looking down at her watch on her right hand, she replies, "Oh, you're right. Thank you." Sarah now turns her attention from the illusive product to packing her bag and gathering her things off her desk to leave for the night. Watching as Sarah collects her items and heads for the door, Mary reminds her to grab her book.

Going back to her desk to retrieve it from the bottom drawer, Sarah says, "Yes, thank you. I forgot it one time two years ago, and I still haven't lived that down."

As Sarah brushes past Mary on her way out the door of her office and heads down the hall toward the elevator, Mary smells a lingering sweet aroma following Sarah. She asks Sarah if she is wearing a new perfume, to which Sarah sheepishly replies, "No," while frantically pushing the down-arrow button as she waits for the elevator. Stepping into the refuge of the elevator, Sarah allows the doors to close behind her before she turns around.

Rita, Another "K" before Book Club

After showing a broker and his client a four-bedroom, five-story walk-up listing in Chelsea, Rita walks them to the door and thanks them for coming this evening. She informs the broker that the apartment has had a lot of action lately, so if they are interested, they need to move quickly because she doesn't think it will stay on the market too much longer. As Rita closes the door behind them and is assured she is alone, she does a little happy dance. "That went really well. I think they might make an offer!" she boasts to herself.

Knowing that her twin teenage sons will be in bed before she gets home tonight, Rita takes out her phone and sends each of them a text. "Hope you are having a good day. My showing went well; I think they will make an offer. Remember to do all your homework and get your gear ready for tomorrow's game. I will be home late tonight because I am meeting the ladies for book club. Good night. Love you." She adds a smiley to the end of her message before hitting send.

Her text is quickly answered with simultaneous responses of "Thanks" from one of her sons and "Have fun with your friends" from the other.

Next Rita texts her husband, Jim. "Hey, so, the showing went well. Cross your fingers they bring an offer. Remember, you have a meeting first thing in the morning at the Birch St. listing. So you might want to make sure you have all the documents you'll need ready tonight. That way you won't need to stop by the office in the morning. I have book club tonight; I will be home late." With hesitation, she adds a heart before hitting send in hope of eliciting a friendly response, remembering they got into another argument earlier that afternoon. She hopes he has had time to cool down by now.

She turns her focus back on her real-estate work at hand, not allowing herself to spend any more time second-guessing who was to blame for today's fight or feeling hurt by how distant Jim has become. Looking through her calendar book and then her texts and e-mails, she meticulously goes through each one, saying, "Check," aloud after each one has been tended to. Once all her work is complete, Rita places her phone in her purse and with a smile on her face is ready to leave the apartment and head for her girls' night out at book club. The very thought of sitting down, relaxing with a glass or two or three or more of wine, and venting with her friends has been the motivation getting her through these last few weeks.

Ten minutes after sending her text to her husband, she receives his response. It's the letter *K*. Just "K," no heart, no "Have fun with the girls," no "Wake me when you get in" with a winky face…just "K." Exhausted from the constant struggles of her marriage, a place where she feels she is the only one apologizing after the fights or making the effort to spark romance in hopes of re-connecting, Rita switches her phone off and drops it back to the bottom of her purse.

⊫＋ ＋⊨

Diane, Predator versus Prey before Rushing to Book Club

The antique shopkeeper's bell hanging from above the door rings as the door to the flower shop opens and a striking young man enters. He is dressed in an outfit that evokes effortless style, with a face that rivals the covers of *GQ* magazine. Petals, the floral shop, is filled with the sweet aroma of fresh flowers. In the center of the shop stands a floor-to-ceiling pyramid of antique pots on display from around the world. The old wooden sills of the windows in the shop show evidence of many layers of paint applied through the years, and the tile floor, made of small white hexagon tiles dappled with black tiles that form a floral pattern, shows the signs of erosion from decades of wear from happy patrons. To the owner of Petals, Diane, the weathered and lived-in look only adds to the shop's charm. Her vision for the shop has always been one of a sanctuary from the busy hustle and bustle of the city streets. It is reminiscent of a shop you might find in the middle of Paris, a place where old-world charm and modern elegance combine to make a beautiful experience. There is an old grandfather clock that sits prominently in the front display window of the shop. It was left there by the previous owner, who ran a clock-repair shop until he retired at the age of eighty-one. Diane didn't have the heart to remove it and admits she loves the history and charm the old clock holds. Petals' character and elegance of times gone by are in sharp contrast to the surrounding storefronts on her block, which are filled with pop-ups and trendy clothing companies.

At the counter both Diane and her assistant, Chad, are standing, looking at a laptop. They are going over the order for an upcoming wedding, for a couple that Diane describes as doomed even before they begin, when they are interrupted by the sound of the bell ringing. Before Diane can get a good look at the customer, Chad leans over and whispers in her ear, "I've got this one."

Knowing that sound in his voice, Diane looks over the top of her glasses to check out the object of affection Chad has spotted. With approval in her voice, she whispers back, "Oh, I see." Then she curiously adds, "Wait, he's only been in the shop for ten seconds. How do you even know he's gay?"

"It only takes a second. It's called gaydar, honey. All gay men have it. It's a gift really," replies Chad in a hushed tone as he fluffs his perfectly coiffed chestnut hair and rounds the corner of the counter to approach the handsome customer.

Diane watches from her desk behind the counter as the hunt begins to unfold, the customer in pursuit of the perfect floral arrangement for a dinner party he will be attending later tonight and Chad in pursuit of the man. She sits in awe, taking in each movement. She watches as the stranger motions in one direction and Chad counters his moves in the other with gentle laughter and the subtle toss of his head, along with the occasional touch of the beautiful man's arm. All the while, Chad is still asking him questions and pointing out flowers. The whole thing has Diane mesmerized. Knowing she could learn a thing or two from him, she considers taking notes, because when Chad is in motion, it's a thing of beauty to watch. He is like a summer storm, a mixture of power and grace.

Twenty minutes later, the hunt has come to an end. Once the innocent prey has left the shop with an armful of flowers and is safely out of sight and ear-shot from the display window, Chad turns to Diane, grinning. Then, gloatingly, he holds up a piece of paper with the handsome stranger's name and number.

Impressed, Diane asks, "How do you do that?"

"It must be my rugged good looks," says Chad, giggling.

"You know what I think? I think you chase them around the shop until they give in from exhaustion," quips Diane.

"Ouch," says Chad, dramatically placing his hand on his heart.

As the old grandfather clock chimes its low seven bongs, Diane gets up from her desk and frantically announces, "It's book-club time!" Fumbling as she collects her things and shuts down her laptop, Diane is flustered. Again, somehow time has gotten away from her. Chad reassures her that he can handle closing the shop and tells her to go have a great time with the ladies as he helps to gather her bag, stopping to look inside to make sure her book is still safely tucked inside before scooting her out the door.

"Thank you. You're right. What would I do without you?" She blows him a kiss and heads out, walking down the street to *Franc's*, which is just right around the corner.

Ali Sweating Off Carbs before Book Club

"Ninety minutes in a hundred and five degrees doing yoga, what the hell was I thinking?" Ali asks herself as she cautiously enters the small room at her gym for her first class of Bikram hot yoga. She is met at the doorway with the gagging smell of sweat and what can only be described as Corn Nuts and feet. However, remembering the motivation for why she is there, she wills herself to enter. In hopes of not making a complete fool out of herself, she lays out her yoga mat in the back row. This way maybe no one will notice she doesn't know the first thing about performing any of the poses. With the stench of sweat still lingering from the previous class like a slice of Stilton blue cheese that has been sitting out in the Sahara Desert for days holding refuge in her nostrils, Ali watches as the others enter the room. She says a little prayer to herself that only women will surround her, with the thought that they may not smell as bad as what she imagines a big hairy man will after an hour and a half of cooking in this heat.

Unfortunately, God was apparently too busy saving lives to hear her plea because as class begins, Ali finds herself looking straight at the wrinkly rear of a man in his late seventies. The older man is wearing a pair of shorts not quite large enough to contain the full girth of his saggy endowment, which now dangles only inches away from her face for what feels like an eternity during most of the poses. The rabbit pose and half-moon with hands to feet are just two of the poses that will now forever be burned into the deepest part of her mind, never to be erased no matter how hard Ali tries. With all the maturity of a fifteen-year-old girl sitting in biology class daydreaming of going all the way with Brad Pitt, Ali's mind begins to wander. Having a front-row seat to the show being displayed in front of her, Ali can't help but be impressed by his ample member. That, of course, is followed by admiration for his wife. "Good for you, sister," she thinks to herself. "Seriously, Ali, you need to get laid." As her admiration for the woman quickly turns to envy, it immediately morphs into repulsion, bringing Ali to shudder at the thought of seeing the man in action. "Gross." However entertaining this random train of thought might be, she knows she needs to pull herself together and stay focused on the poses being asked of her from the instructor. "Come on, focus, Ali," she silently demands of herself. Then she sternly adds, "Stop looking around the room and breathe. Focus on a frickin' serene, peaceful place."

As class drones on, Ali finds that with each changing pose, she is getting more and more dizzy. She wonders if it's from the repulsive stench, the dangling gonads, or the heat? Her only comfort from her nausea comes from the reparative silent rants and curses directed at her boss. She continues to secretly chant them over and over again, creating a sort of personal mantra to keep from passing out from what she self-diagnoses as heatstroke and dehydration. Combating the pain created by contorting her body in gravity-defying positions with the thought of telling off her producer (if only in her daydreams) puts an instant smile on Ali's face. However, to completely ease the discomfort of being locked in a room absent of fresh air and getting to know the old man in front of her in ways only dogs can relate, she believes it may take something a little stronger, like a pitcher of margaritas, to erase today's events.

Dragging her limp body to the locker room for a cool shower after the exhausting workout, Ali feels proud of herself for toughing it through and completing the class. In spite of her self-proclaimed accolades, she has no illusions of attending another hot yoga class again anytime in the near future. She thinks instead, "Maybe next week I will try Zumba. Dancing around in front of a mirror to hip-hop, how bad can that be?" An hour later, she is primped, refreshed, and ready to join her friends at *Franc's* for tonight's book-club gathering. "Dehydration and wine should pair well together," she thinks.

Riding in the cab on her way to *Franc's*, she has visions of what she is going to order: bread, lots of bread, gooey mac and cheese, and a huge chunk of that glorious chocolate decadence that Brenda makes so well. The mere thought of food makes her stomach ache and start to growl. The sound is so loud that at times she is sure the cab driver can hear it. And sure enough, after the next animal sound reverberates through her stomach, she catches the driver's eye in the rearview mirror looking at her. Embarrassed, Ali smiles sheepishly back at him and folds her arms across her belly, attempting to muffle the grumbling.

⊷⊶

Kathy in the Morning of Book Club

Kathy makes her way down the creaky wooden staircase that leads to the foyer of her row house in Brooklyn. She sees through the hall to the kitchen that her husband, Ed, is already there making them both breakfast. As she walks down the long hallway toward the kitchen, the smell of fresh coffee brewing puts a smile on her face. She crosses the black-and-white-checkered kitchen floor to the cupboard and pulls out two matching mugs. The mugs are from Caesars in Atlantic City. They bought them as souvenirs last summer when they stayed at the casino to celebrate their thirty-seventh wedding anniversary.

Atlantic City has always held a special place for both of them because it was there that Kathy first found out that she was pregnant with their oldest son, Caleb. They had decided to go to the casino for the long Labor Day weekend. Ed had just placed his bet at the roulette table when, without warning, Kathy projectile vomited across the game and the dealer. It was true she had been feeling nauseous all day, but she thought it was the clam chowder she had had earlier for lunch. The thought of being pregnant had never entered her mind. They had tried to get pregnant for so many years and had come to believe it would never happen. However, when the nausea continued into the third day, Kathy decided to stop by the hotel's lobby and ask for directions to the nearest pharmacy. To her relief, there was one six blocks away.

Not wanting to get Ed's hopes up only to disappoint him, as she had done so many times before, Kathy decided to sneak away to the store while Ed was distracted at the blackjack tables. Battling the 101-degree weather and humidity, Kathy made her way to the store. Nauseous from what ailed her and sweating from her journey, Kathy frantically searched the aisles for a pregnancy test. Once at the checkout counter, she was overcome with hope, so she decided to take the test at the store. Engulfing the seat with layers of toilet paper, Kathy carefully unwrapped the stick and performed the test. A minute and a lifetime later, Kathy found the answer she had dreamed of for so long staring back at her; she was finally going to be a mom.

Remembering that special trip, she smiles each time she looks at the mugs. Kathy pours them both coffees before sitting at their weathered antique kitchen table. Ed finishes the scrambled eggs with wheat toast and sets Kathy's plate in front of her and then takes a seat next to her with his own before noticing the look of anxiety beginning to come across Kathy's face. Reaching over and placing his right hand on hers, he reassures her that everything will be okay and adds that it will all work out. She gives him a shaky smile and says, "I hope you are right, but I'm not so sure. You know how I can get sometimes, especially if it's something I really believe in."

"Oh, trust me. I am well aware of how stubborn you can be when you think you're right," eagerly agrees Ed.

Kathy quickly returns, "Well, I don't think. I know I am right about this. If you only knew how bad things have gotten. I am really worried that the nurses may go on strike. And, I mean, who could really blame them? They are getting the short end of the stick. It isn't fair."

Sympathizing with his wife's dilemma, Ed adds, "Yes, I know you are just looking out for your nurses, but remember you can't go into today's meeting ready to fight. You need to listen to what they are proposing. I know you feel passionate about protecting your staff. One of the things I love most about you is your compassion, but you have to remain professional."

Conceding to the wisdom of her husband, she says, "All right, I'll try to play nice in the meeting, but I can't guarantee anything."

"That's all I'm asking," replies Ed.

After breakfast, Kathy rinses their plates before placing them in the sink, along with the pan and mugs. Leaving together, they head for Ed's car. As they are pulling out of their driveway, he tells Kathy he forgot to tell her that the mechanic called and said her car should be fixed by next Tuesday. She is relieved by the news that she will soon be getting her car back but also a little sad that their morning routine will soon go back to normal, thinking that it has been nice sharing their mornings and ride into work together.

While crossing the bridge into the city, Kathy reminds Ed that she won't need to be picked up from work today because today is the day she starts physical therapy, and then afterward she'll just catch a cab from the hospital to *Franc's* for book club. Driving along their commute, the two joke about Kathy starting physical therapy. She is clearly anxious about how long it's been since she has exercised, much less seen the inside of a gym. As they pull up in front of the hospital, she looks over toward Ed, smiles, and jests, "Will you still find me irresistible when I have the body of a supermodel?"

Pulling her close to him, he kisses her dramatically and says in his best Rhett Butler impersonation, "Frankly, my dear, I don't give a damn. I will always find you irresistible."

Loving the attention he shows her, Kathy pushes him away flirtatiously and replies, "You know you're crazy, right?"

"Yeah, since the day I met you," Ed says, grinning.

Amid the smiles and jokes, Kathy unfortunately notices the time glaring at her from the clock on the radio and knows it is time for her to go into work. Reluctant to leave the comfort of their car and her husband, Kathy looks at the hospital, pauses, and takes a deep breath before exiting the car with her book safely tucked away in her new gym bag. But, before she gets out of ear shot, Ed tries one more time to lighten her mood by shouting from the car, "Have fun at book club tonight. Tell the girls I said hi."

"Ahh, book club!" Just the thought of it brings a smile to Kathy's face.

CHAPTER 4

THURSDAY MORNING
AT FRANC'S

Franc arrives at the restaurant just before nine in the morning, as she does every morning. Making her way through the kitchen and back to the office, she stops to say good morning to her manager, who is waiting for her with a stack of papers in his hand. She also says a quick hello to the prep chefs and her head chef and brother-in-law, Roman.

Chef Roman has been working here for years. He started in the back, washing dishes, and through the years has climbed the ladder to become one of the city's finest chefs. When Roman was younger and new to the restaurant, Franc's dad saw potential in him. He was intelligent, punctual, polite, and very eager to learn.

So when Roman came to him and said he wanted to one day be a chef, Franc's dad was thrilled. Over time, her dad transitioned Roman from his dishwashing duties to the kitchen line. There Roman worked side by side with her father and the other chefs, learning as he shadowed them each night. Roman felt grateful for the opportunity to learn a new technique or master a new skill and soon came to realize that no task was too menial; he grew to understand that a successful kitchen is the result of the cohesive marriage of all the kitchen help. Roman asked lots of questions and took careful mental notes on how the chefs used their instincts and knowledge to create the most amazing dishes. Working so closely together for so many years, Franc's father began to think of Roman as the son he never had, which at the time was something Franc envied, but now has come to understand. Her father encouraged Roman to attend culinary school part-time and made adjustments in his work schedule so as not to interfere with his classes. He even helped Roman with some of the expenses of school, with the agreement that Roman would continue to stay on at Franc's after graduation. This arrangement came with the knowledge that he was being groomed to take over as head chef when the time came for Franc's dad to retire.

The one thing Franc's dad did not account for when he met Roman for the first time so many years ago was the marriage between him and his oldest daughter, Gina. Their romance developed slowly over time. Perhaps it was a natural progression of spending so much time together at the restaurant, not to mention the constant encouragement from her nosey mother, Sophia. It was only right that Gina, being the oldest, wed first, according to their mother's logic. The wedding was a monumental event for the family and therefore made the nuptials of Luke and Laura on *General Hospital* pale in comparison. Like most things in the eighties, the bigger the better, and this was no exception. Gina's headpiece, made of billowing yards of tulle, fake pearls, and rhinestones, was so large that the sheer weight of it made her strain to keep it upright during the ceremony. Franc and her three other sisters wore teal-blue bridesmaid dresses with matching headpieces that weren't much better, just smaller. The wedding dress, with its exaggerated puffy shoulders and long train, made maneuvering down the aisle an Olympic event for her sister.

Gina's wedding to Roman was just the beginning. Her three other sisters, Theresa, Maria, and Veronica, followed suit one by one over the next few years, leaving Franc the unobstructed focus of her mom's matchmaking attention. Sophia's quest to find her daughter a husband has become her full-time job and Franc's nightmare. She knows her mom's intentions are good, but her actions can sometimes be exhausting to say the least.

Following behind Franc this morning, through the kitchen to her office, is her manager, Derek. Derek is tall and uncommonly handsome, not the kind of man you look at and immediately think, "Wow," but the kind of man who grows on you slowly like a fine wine. He has kind eyes and an engaging smile. His thick, dark hair is beginning to show signs of gray, and the lines framing his eyes convey wisdom and age. Derek has a nine-year-old daughter named Maddy, whom he shares custody of with his ex-wife, Lori. They were high-school sweethearts, dated all through college, and married shortly thereafter. Derek has worked in many restaurants over the years. In his third year of college, he took on a second job at a local bar on the weekends to help with the mounting cost of tuition and to save money for his future with Lori. He's always been a hard worker and thrives on the fast pace and diversity that come with the restaurant lifestyle.

Shortly after their marriage, they decided to throw caution to the wind and open their own diner. Lori found a job in her field of education while Derek spent those early years trying to build the diner's business. Unfortunately, before too long the hours and constant challenges of the struggling diner began to consume all his time. The extensive work hours Derek kept each day began to take a toll on their marriage. More often than not, Lori fell asleep long before Derek came home from the diner, and she spent most weekends alone while

Derek ran to the diner to address one thing or another. As the years went by, their happy marriage started to show signs of struggle and regret. Derek's dedication to his work took first position, which left little time for his marriage. The strong work ethic Lori once admired in Derek quickly turned to the one thing they fought about most. What had once been a playful marriage turned into something filled with arguments and familiar routines rather than passion and romance.

In an attempt to rekindle a long-forgotten spark in their marriage, they decided to have a baby and were blessed with a precious little girl nine months later. They tried hard to focus their attention on parenting rather than their mundane marriage. Things at first were great; they spent lots of time together, bonding and caring for Maddy, but that too would change. It didn't take long for Derek to fall back into his workaholic ways of putting the diner first. When Maddy was three, they decided to divorce. They've been able to remain close friends, not just for Maddy's sake, but because they both cherish the time they have spent together, the history of memories made and lives lived with each other. Within a couple of years, the small diner he had worked so hard to create and sacrificed so much of himself for would eventually close due to the economic strains of the times, a fate that led him in time to *Franc's.*

Over the years Lori has brought Maddy into *Franc's* many times for dinner, and sometimes on Derek's days off, he stops in with her to finish a quick errand or two. On occasions when Derek is busy doing paperwork or talking to vendors, Franc takes Maddy to her office where they can visit over one of the pastry chef, Brenda's, delicious desserts and a mug of hot chocolate. It's during these times that Franc has really come to know and care for Maddy. Franc may not be a mom herself, but the years spent being Aunt Francie to her growing number of nieces and nephews have given her lots of experience with children. Maddy's a very talkative nine-year-old. Sometimes they talk about school, and other times they discuss a new TV show or movie or music. Although Franc has to admit most of the time she doesn't know whom or what show Maddy is referring to or the song she is excited about. So usually after she leaves, Franc takes a few minutes to look them up on Google—that way the next time Maddy is in, she can add something to the conversation. Watching Maddy run around the stockroom or hang out in the kitchen with her nieces and nephews reminds Franc of her own childhood growing up here at the restaurant. At times she watches as Maddy stands at the front hostess station, helping Sophia greet each customer, and it takes her back to when she was younger. Franc can still remember how excited she felt watching the door to see who was coming and how happy she was to witness as her mom's friendly smile and warm demeanor made each customer feel special.

Derek has been with the restaurant for about five years, and in those years Franc can't remember him taking a day of sick leave. He is always eager to please and constantly sports a grin on his face. Not much slows Derek down. She has to admit sometimes his sunshine-and-rainbow attitude can be a little hard to take early in the morning, especially before her first shot of caffeine. However, Franc will concede there is something she finds very appealing about this man, but she hasn't quite figured out exactly what it is yet. Nor can she stop herself from feeling flushed each time he stands near to her.

In spite of Franc's intrigue, she has made it a rule to never get romantically involved with anyone in her restaurant. Unfortunately, this is a rule that became a little blurred one night for Derek and herself. It was at the restaurant's New Year's Eve celebration when Franc found herself feeling lonely and sorry for herself, for once again she would be ringing in the New Year alone—feelings that clearly contributed to her overconsumption of champagne and the unplanned kiss that took place in her office at the stroke of midnight. The next morning, she woke to a wicked headache, her stomach in knots, and her thoughts racing: "Oh shit! What have I done? This isn't okay. I'm his boss. Ugh! This can't happen. It's too complicated. I need to keep the lines clearly drawn between boss and lover. And what if things don't work out between us? The fallout after a breakup could be not only awkward but damaging to the restaurant. I've got to put a stop to this today."

That was over a year and a half ago, and despite having dated other men, Franc sometimes still catches herself distracted by Derek's warm smile and the memory of that kiss, that one *weak in the knees, forget your own name* kiss. She remembers every detail, the electricity that ran through her body that night in her office as he pinned her up against the wall. She remembers the way he held her hands firmly down by her sides and leaned sternly against her body, allowing his weight and the heat from his chest to penetrate hers. She remembers the way he slowly tilted his head and kissed her warmly on the mouth, parting his lips until his tongue met hers. Next he began to kiss the length of her collarbone, allowing his teeth to nibble her softly, causing all her skin to respond from the current running through her body. She remembers thinking how she didn't want things to stop as he made his way up her neck toward her right ear. She remembers the heat of his breath and the way his lips felt as they grazed her earlobe when he began to whisper what she thought was going to be an invitation to continue their encounter elsewhere. But to her disappointment, he instead said in a sultry voice, "I've called you a cab. It should be here shortly. Get home safely, beautiful. I'll see you in the morning." Then he walked away, leaving her standing there alone in the office, melting, craving for him to turn around and come back and finish the job he had started.

This morning, however, is a much different scene. Derek takes a seat across the desk from Franc as she puts her bag down and hangs her coat on the back of her chair before sitting. Never skipping a beat, Derek with business on his mind hands her a pile of papers and dives into the numbers from last night for both the dining room and bar. Then he hands Franc the invoices from today's shipment, along with tonight's menu and number of reservations. A few moments into her meeting with Derek, the pastry chef, Brenda, comes in carrying Franc's morning pick-me-up, consisting of a strong cup of espresso and two cannolis, which she places down in front of Franc with a smile. One sip of the espresso and she can already feel her eyes start to open wider and her brain begin to fire up. Once they've finished going over the numbers, Derek leaves to assemble the staff in the dining room for the morning meeting. This gives Franc a few minutes to finish her breakfast and review the reservation schedule for today's guests. She looks for any notes her mother may have put next to the guests' names. It's important to know if someone is coming in to celebrate a special occasion, such as an anniversary or birthday. That way when they arrive, they are met with the proper greeting, and Franc can have Brenda prepare a little something special for their dessert or have a bottle of bubbly sent to their table.

Today one reservation stands out to her among all the others. It's the third Thursday of the month, and for *Franc's* that means it is book-club night. The thought of seeing these ladies always puts a smile on her face. Through the years this group has become some of her favorite customers. She never knows what inappropriately funny thing they will be talking about when she approaches the table or what crazy outfit Melissa is going to show up wearing. Before leaving the office to join the staff, Franc takes a moment to look over at the photo of her dad and grandfather and chuckles. "It is going to be a crazy night!"

By the time she reaches the dining room, Derek has assembled all the staff. Franc goes over the usual things, like the dinner specials and how many customers they are expecting to have tonight based on the reservations and estimated walk-ins. She makes a point to remind Sophia that they will be having the book-club ladies back tonight and that she needs to be sure to reserve their usual booth. Franc also lets the waitstaff know they have a new waitress on tonight, saying, "Tonight is Megan's first night of waitressing, so she may need a little help. Please, step in and lend a hand if you see she is in trouble. All right, I think that's everything. Let's have a great night, people, and remember to treat every customer like they are family."

CHAPTER 5

THE LADIES OF BOOK CLUB ARRIVE AT FRANC'S

It is eight o'clock on the third Thursday in April. The evening is chilly, but the fragrant cherry blossoms flowering outside the restaurant hold the promise of warmer days to come. Kathy's cab pulls up in front of a swanky Italian restaurant in the heart of Manhattan. With a smile on her face, she exits the cab and enters the building knowing tonight will be filled with laughter and bonding with her favorite girlfriends over great food and an endless, free-flowing river of wine...*and* after the day she just had at the hospital, between working in the ER and attending physical therapy, she feels more ready for book club than ever.

Tonight, like most nights of the week, *Franc's* lobby is filled with people dressed in city-chic attire, waiting for their tables. Some of the patrons are waiting for their reservations, while others are there in hopes of grabbing a cancellation. Kathy and her group of ladies have been going to *Franc's* on the third Thursday of every month for the past ten years. It is because of this that she knows her table will be waiting for her. So rather than politely waiting her turn to approach the hostess, Kathy wades through the crowd and walks directly to the podium, ignoring the many looks of annoyance coming from the hungry customers. There, she is greeted by name and immediately shown to her table by Sophia, the restaurant's main hostess. Dressed in a simple black sheath with tasteful black pumps, Sophia looks as elegant as always. With her glittery silver hair twisted neatly in a bun, her signature red lips, and her piercing blue eyes, Franc's mother's beauty is as bountiful as her romantic heart, friendly demeanor, and curiosity. All admirable attributes—however, in spite of her best intentions, they can sometimes get the better of her.

"Aw, Kathy, it is so nice to see you again," says Sophia warmly as she closes her hands together near her heart in a show of gratitude.

"Thanks, Sophia, it's nice to see you too," replies Kathy, adding a friendly smile.

Walking to the table, the familiar hostess directs her guest. "Right this way. We have your table ready." Then she adds, "You are the first one here tonight."

She escorts Kathy to a large booth covered in distressed dark saddle leather, located in the center of the restaurant. Just like the restaurant, the tablescapes are sophisticated with a touch of glamour. Each table is topped with a crisp white linen, two candles in hurricanes adorned with crystals, and orange tulips arranged in a silver-footed vase. The restaurant is dimly lit, allowing the candlelight to flood the room with a warm glow, and the oversize crystals hanging from the chandeliers dotted across the ceiling and dangling from the sconces along the walls add a glitter to the room much like a fine piece of jewelry that completes the perfect outfit.

Kathy, looking around the bustling dining room filled with happy people, thanks Sophia for showing her to the booth and comments, "Looks like another busy night."

Sophia brings her pinched right hand to her mouth and blows a kiss into the air in true Italian form. "Francisco would be so proud of his little girl. God rest his soul." Then she makes the symbol of the cross over her chest.

"I am sure he is," comforts Kathy.

Sophia's natural curiosity surrounding Kathy's job soon takes over. "So tell me, how are things at the hospital? Did you get any real weirdoes in lately? You see the craziest things down there in the ER. Anyone come in with a sex injury or a limb falling off from some rare flesh-eating disease? You can tell me. I can keep a secret," says Sophia eagerly.

"No," says Kathy, laughing. "Nothing nearly that exciting."

Looking back toward the lobby, Sophia can see Franc greeting customers while looking around the dining room to see where she has run off to. "Oops, I see my daughter's at the podium. I've got to go. She doesn't like it when I spend so much time with the guests. She says I can be a bit intrusive."

"Oh, don't listen to her. I think you're wonderful. Besides, I think it's nice that you take the time to get to know your customers," Kathy assures her warmly.

Sophia replies quickly, "I'll be sure to tell her you said that." Then she smiles and walks back to her position at the front of the restaurant.

Since she is the first to arrive, Kathy seats herself in the center of the booth and places her book next to her on the seat. Moments later she looks up to see Rita walking toward the table. Rita is wearing what has become her uniform—black pants, a white shirt, and a black blazer. Happy to see another member of book club, Kathy smiles and gives a small wave to Rita as she approaches.

Rita sits down to the right of Kathy and places her book on the back of the tufted banquette before asking, "So how was your day?"

Kathy sarcastically replies, "Oh, just another day in paradise. How about you? Did you get the Brookses' place sold?"

Rita lets out a sigh. "Finally. We close on the thirtieth. Thank God. I swear if I have to listen to Mrs. Brooks go on one more time about needing a large bonus room for her precious grandkids to play in, I am going to shoot myself. How can anyone be that stupid? I've met her precious grandkids, and they are nowhere close to the angels she thinks they are. I know I shouldn't talk so badly about kids, but I swear they are obnoxious, spoiled brats. Truly, the spawns of Satan!"

Kathy chuckles. "Well, I work with those kids' father, and, yep, spawn of Satan pretty much sums him up too."

Despite the wildly underparented grandkids, Rita tells Kathy that she sincerely appreciates the referral. She adds that she hasn't come this far in the Manhattan real-estate world without dealing with a few unruly clients, and by now she knows how to handle them and whatever or whomever they throw her way.

Melissa arrives next at *Franc's*. She is wearing a gold top, a headband with sequined leopard print, dark-brown skinny jeans, and ankle-high stiletto boots. When she is escorted over to the table, Melissa greets Kathy and Rita with the usual air kisses and then places her tattered book on the table as she sits down in the booth and begins to slide to the left of Kathy. Just then a very young blond waitress, with her hair pulled tightly away from her face, walks over to the ladies' table. She is wearing the restaurant waitstaff's strict uniform of black pants, a white tailored shirt, a man's tie, and a white apron.

The young lady begins to introduce herself, saying, "Hi, ladies, I'm Megan, and I will be your server this evening. I see we are still waiting for some others to arrive. Can I get anyone started with a beverage while you wait?"

Kathy is first to answer. "I'll take the house chardonnay from Napa."

The waitress talks to herself while writing the drink on her order pad: "One glass of chardonnay." Then she looks toward Rita. "And for you?"

Before Rita can answer, Kathy interrupts, "A bottle, not a glass."

Embarrassed by her mistake, the waitress replies, "Oh, sorry." Then she turns to leave while making the corrections to their order on her notepad, assuming the ladies are going to share the bottle.

Rita, impatiently waiting to place her order as the waitress turns to walk away, says, "I will have one too."

Confused by the ladies' attitude and drink order, Megan answers, "Oh, okay. I will bring you a glass as well."

Annoyed that the waitress does not know their routine, Rita interjects, "No, I'll have a bottle of chardonnay."

A look of confusion is now on the waitress's face as she questions what she has just heard. "A bottle?"

Happy to think the waitress is catching on to their orders, Melissa smiles and says, "Make mine the house merlot from Tuscany."

"You want a bottle of the house merlot and two bottles of the chardonnay?" asks the waitress while clearly doing the math in her head, three ladies and three bottles of wine.

Kathy says with disdain, "Don't judge us. Just bring us the damn bottles."

As the waitress walks away, Rita looks at Kathy and rolls her eyes. "She's probably new."

Kathy smirks. "Just my luck."

Coming out of the kitchen, Franc can hear and see the situation starting to unfold at the table with the book-club ladies. It is clear from the look on Megan's face that she is completely confused, while Kathy looks as if she is about to educate poor Megan on how to do her job. Guessing what must have happened, she can't help but giggle a little to herself. "Oh Lord, I bet the ladies tried to place their wine orders." Franc rushes over as quickly as she can to save the struggling waitress, mumbling along the way, "Who put her on table nine? I told the staff to look out for her tonight; she's not ready for those kinds of customers."

By the time she reaches the table, Megan is just standing there looking like a deer caught in headlights. Politely, Franc relieves the new waitress of her duties.

"It's okay, Megan. I've got this. Why don't you go see if table seven needs more bread?"

Turning her attention now toward the table, Franc apologizes, "Sorry, ladies, she's new."

Melissa, with the kindness of a mother, replies, "We thought so, but hey, everyone has to start a new job at some point. Really, she was sweet." She pauses before adding, "She's just not that sharp, if you know what I mean."

Franc wishes she could reply with, "Yes, I know exactly what you mean," and explain that the only reason she hired Megan, a girl with no prior waitressing experience, in the first place was because she was doing a favor for her older sister, Veronica. Megan's mom, Jeninne, and Veronica have been friends since college. Jeninne expressed to her friend how worried she was about her daughter moving to New York. So, Veronica asked if Franc would keep an eye on Megan by letting her work in the restaurant. Like so many young kids with hopes of becoming the next big thing to hit Broadway, Megan left her school in Pennsylvania to pursue a career in acting in the Big Apple. Unfortunately, not only is Megan lacking in waitressing skills, but from what Franc's heard from Veronica, her acting skills aren't much better." However, instead of broadcasting the young girl's shortcomings, Franc instead quickly changes the subject.

"Thank you for coming in tonight. I have to tell you I look forward to seeing you ladies all month. You always manage to put a smile on my face and give me great insights to think about." She takes all but one of the beverage lists from the table. "Don't worry. I will take care of this for you. I'll be right back with your wines." Knowing the ladies as well as Franc does, there is no need to ask them for their drink orders because they always have the same thing.

Next to arrive for tonight's book club is Diane. Ready to greet spring in all its glory, Diane is dressed in a pale-blue dress with a pair of fuchsia Manolo Blahniks and carries her book in a canary-yellow leather tote. As she passes Franc on her way to the table, Diane gives her wine order. Afterward, Diane continues on her way to the waiting table which is already happily buzzing with laughter from her friends.

While at the bar retrieving the bottles, Franc comments to Joe, who is tending the bar this evening, "I'll be seeing you a lot tonight." She pauses to motion in the direction of the ladies. "It's book-club night."

Smiling, Joe replies, "Cool, I love it when they come in. You never know what's going to happen."

"I know, right? They do keep things interesting." Taking the bottles from Joe, she looks back toward the table and notices that before Diane can take her seat next to Melissa, Kathy asks everyone to scoot out of the booth. Apparently she needs to use the restroom. Franc chuckles to the bartender and moves her head in the ladies' direction. "I see the game of musical chairs has begun."

"What? Already? They just got here," states the bartender.

Ali arrives at *Franc's* next and eagerly walks up to the table. She looks striking in a cashmere charcoal wrap, skinny white jeans, and tall black boots. As she sits down next to Rita, she immediately starts complaining about being hungry.

"Well, hello to you too?" snarks Melissa from across the table, trying to be funny.

"Sorry, you know how I get. Yes, hello, ladies. How is everyone doing?" asks Ali apologetically. Then she turns toward Rita and hands off her coffee-stained book. Rita then places it on top of her own book on the back of the banquette. Just as they are all getting settled in their seats, Kathy returns from the bathroom, and the whole booth shuffle has to start all over again. Once the ladies are again settled into their places, Ali looks around the room, sighs, and says with a smile of true euphoria on her face, "This is the one night of the month that I can eat and drink anything I want. No guilt, just gluttony and carbs. Man, I love book club." This statement of truth of course brings everyone to laughter.

Catching a glimpse of Bette as she enters *Franc's*, Kathy is brought to an uncharacteristic silence. The ladies all turn to see what has stolen her attention. Shocked by what they see, they are now all speechless. Its Bette dressed in *Leave It to Beaver* June Cleaver attire, complete with gloves and pearls, with her book clutched in her arms like a schoolgirl. As she makes her way to the table, with a swing in her step, the tapping of her heels on the hardwood floor makes music all its own… tap, tap, tap…Her pencil skirt allows for minimal movement as she walks with short, quick steps…tap, tap, tap. "Sorry. Sorry, ladies, I'm late," she says as she reaches the table and takes her seat next to Ali.

Stunned by the transformation from bohemian chic to downright 1950s housewife, no one says a thing back to her. They just continue to stare in awe, mesmerized by the change and not really sure what to say.

Delivering the bottles of wine to the table, Franc breaks the deafening silence by asking Bette if she'd like her usual. "A bottle of Syrah for you tonight, Bette?"

"Thanks, Franc, but not tonight. Tonight I feel like a sidecar," replies Bette with a twinkle in her eye.

Looking over at Ali, Franc asks, "And what about you, Ali? A bottle of cabernet sauvignon?"

Barely letting Franc finish speaking, Ali happily interjects, "Oh yeah…"

Franc, too, is surprised by tonight's new appearance and can't help but shake her head in disbelief as she walks away from the table and travels back to the bar.

Trying desperately not to appear rude by continuing to stare and bring more attention to the sudden transformation, Rita attempts to act normal. Turning toward Bette, she starts a conversation. "We missed you last month. How was the writers' convention in Vegas? Did you win big?"

"Oh, you could say that," replies Bette with a sly grin.

Suddenly, without warning, Ali lets out a fart. Not a ladylike, demure passing of gas, but a full-out earth-shaking man's fart.

"Are you kidding me? Thanks for the warm welcoming, Ali," says Bette sarcastically.

Diane, repulsed by the smell, exclaims, "Good Lord, Ali!"

"My eyes, they're burning," complains Melissa dramatically.

"Sorry, it's this new diet that I am on," says Ali with a sheepish grin. "I can't help it. It's like my intestines have a mind of their own; no warning, just deadly fire."

Rita interjects, "I don't care how much weight you lose, honey; it's not worth it."

Last to arrive to tonight's gathering is Sarah. As she passes by the hostess podium, she stops to say a quick hello to Sophia before heading to join her friends already seated at their usual booth. She looks amazing tonight in a nude-colored pencil skirt and brown stilettos with her book neatly tucked away in her olive Stella McCartney handbag. However, by the look on her face, she is clearly a little flustered. She apologizes for being late even before she takes her seat next to Diane.

From across the room at the bar, Franc notices Sarah's arrival to the table. Knowing her order, she returns to the table with Bette's sidecar and a dirty martini with three olives for Sarah. Not wanting to interrupt the group, she drops off the drinks without saying a word. However, Sarah makes a point to make eye contact with her before she has the chance to walk away. Franc then watches as Sarah takes a sip of the martini.

"Mmm." Sarah smiles. "Aw. Thank you. This is just what I needed."

"I thought you looked like you needed one of these tonight," replies Franc quietly with a nod of understanding before walking back to the kitchen to check in with Roman and Derek. It's supposed to be a full house again tonight, and she wants to make sure things are running smoothly.

PART TWO

Orders Are Taken

CHAPTER 6

SOPHIA'S BEAUTY ADVICE

Franc

As Franc makes her way back to the kitchen to retrieve a bread basket for the book-club table, she is met by her mother, who's thrilled to offer the latest restaurant drama. Sophia wants to let her know that a table of young women has just arrived and is seated at table twelve. Without skipping a beat, she dives into their story. "They're here for dinner, and then they're going 'clubbing,'" she says, using air quotes to emphasize her excitement. "They're here to start Chloe's bachelorette party for dinner before going out. I told them I thought it was smart of them to get a good meal in before heading out to wherever it is you young people go. Back in my day, women didn't do such things. No one had bachelorette parties. Men on the other hand

and your father, well, now that's a whole other story. You should have seen—"

Seeing that her mother is about to go on a tangent, Franc tries to reel her in. "Mom, what about table twelve?"

Back on track, Sophia continues, saying, "Right, anyway, Becka—that's the one with red hair—never thought Chloe would ever find someone, and now look at her. She's about to marry a doctor—a doctor, Frances!"

"And you got all of that from escorting them to their table," Franc says, impressed by her mom's ability to get people to open up to her.

"What can I say? People like to talk," answers Sophia. "You know, maybe if you tried a little harder, you too could find yourself a nice doctor to settle down with."

"Mom, we aren't having this conversation again," she replies for the umpteenth time.

Putting her hand to Franc's forehead, Sophia begins brushing away her bangs, adding, "Maybe you should try putting on a little eye shadow to highlight your beautiful brown eyes. I'll pick some up tomorrow while I'm at the market. You'll like it."

"Mom, stop," Franc says, annoyed, moving her mom's hand away from her face.

"A little lipstick wouldn't hurt either," continues Sophia without skipping a beat. "You look pale. A little color would look nice." Pointing to her own lips, she says, "See." Then she asks, "Whatever happened to the one I left on your desk? I don't see you wear it." Not waiting for a reply, Sophia adds, "No worries, I will pick up another one when I'm out getting your eye shadow."

As Franc grabs the bread basket, she says with exhaustion, "Mom, I'm fine. I don't need anything."

"Who said anything about need? I'm just trying to enhance what God already gave you," defends her mother.

Just then Franc notices Derek standing by the door, getting an earful. Unfortunately, before he can escape, Sophia sees him too and innocently asks, "Derek, don't you think Frances would look lovely with just a little pop of color on her lips?"

Not knowing where this conversation might lead, he replies cautiously, with a smile, "Um, I don't know. I think she looks perfect just the way she is," then walks by Franc on his way to the pantry, but not before letting his fingertips graze the back of her hand as he brushes past.

Annoyed by the conversation with her mother and flustered from the electricity that is now running through her body from Derek's subtle touch, Franc frantically heads out the door to the dining room with her bread basket in hand. Catching her breath as the door to the kitchen closes behind her, Franc is once again finding it hard to stick to her rule of keeping things professional between Derek and her. Lately, it seems more often than not her brain and her loins have been at war...*and* it looks as though her loins might be winning.

CHAPTER 7

KATHY AND THE MERGER

Delivering the warm basket of homemade bread to the book-club group, Franc is immediately met with gratitude from Ali. As Ali takes the warm basket from her hand before it has a chance to touch the table, she sticks her head over the steam and sighs. "Yum." She then takes a bite and makes a moan reminiscent of what usually only takes place late at night in the bedroom.

"Is it too cliché to say, 'I'll have what she's having'?" says Diane, chuckling.

The only reply Franc can muster is, "Me too, sister," before quickly walking away from the table blushing.

Flushed with embarrassment, Ali replies, "Sorry, but they are so good. I can't help it."

"How's the merger coming along?" asks Rita, looking toward Kathy. "Are you guys any closer to getting things wrapped up?"

"No, not really. I'm afraid this is going to drag out forever," answers Kathy, exhausted from her day at the hospital.

Sarah responds with a sympathetic tone, "Well, hopefully they'll find a solution soon."

"That would take someone other than the moron they've got running the show," answers Kathy. "Seriously, some days I don't know why I even get out of bed."

Melissa says cheerfully, "Come on. Your day couldn't have been that bad."

"Oh, trust me. It was," answers Kathy without hesitation.

⊨⊨ ⊨⊨

Kathy and the Hospital

Entering the hospital's crowded emergency room, Kathy makes her way around the front desk while greeting the nurses manning the station. She lets them know she has another meeting this morning but will be on the floor after it's over. Walking down the hall, which is made of white tiles randomly scattered with primary colors and walls adorned with watercolor landscapes, Kathy is met by a nurse before she has a chance to reach her office. The nurse is clearly upset with the new regulations and schedules that the hospital has been implementing. Kathy reassures her that she will look into it and asks her to tell the others that she'll do her best to keep things running as smoothly as possible during this transitional period.

Kathy barely makes it to her office and takes off her jacket before a coworker comes in and asks, "Hey, are you ready?"

Kathy smiles, raises an eyebrow, and replies with a noticeable lack of enthusiasm, "I guess."

They leave her office and walk down the hall together to catch the elevator. They are both headed to the fifth-floor boardroom, along with the other heads of departments and board members. As the meeting begins, Kathy notices that there are only two seats left at the large oval conference table. One seat is by the chief of staff, Geoffrey Brooks, and the other by the head of radiology, a woman they all "lovingly" refer to behind her back as "Smellin' Helen." Knowing she would rather sit by Helen and hold her breath than sit by the chief and hold her tongue, Kathy smiles at Helen and makes a move for the seat. Unfortunately, before she can reach the open chair, Mark from neurology takes the open spot. Reluctantly, Kathy retreats and takes her place next to the hospital's chief of staff. Looking up at Kathy as she takes her seat, Geoffrey greets her with a nervous smile. In years past, she and the chief have had a great working relationship, and she would even consider him a friend. However, since the impending merger, she is finding it harder to tread the line between friendship and work with him. "Good morning, Chief," replies Kathy. "This should be interesting."

"Kathy," says the chief, with concern in his voice.

"What? I'm not going to do anything," answers Kathy, looking as innocent as a child with her hand caught in the cookie jar.

Tensions in the room run high as the attorney facilitating the merger informs them all in great detail about more budget cuts and impending job losses in the near future. Kathy, like many of the others in the room, is clearly upset by this topic. Unfortunately for her, she seems to be the one having the hardest time concealing her frustration, as displayed by her fidgeting, eye rolling, and exaggerated exhaling. Her department, as well as many others, has already experienced budget cuts to the point of affecting the hospital's ability to serve its patients adequately.

After yet another ignorant statement from the facilitator, Kathy clears her throat loudly and makes a gesture conveying she is about to speak her mind, when, to her utter shock, the chief of staff kicks her in the shin under the table. With pain radiating up her leg, she quickly turns to him, ready to question his actions. However, the look on his face gives her a clear signal to keep her mouth shut.

As the meeting comes to an end, everyone, including Kathy, is all too eager to leave the room. Moving as a herd, they walk away, visibly angry and discouraged by what's been discussed, grumbling with one another as they make their ways back to their departments. Down the corridor, Geoffrey catches up to Kathy and pulls her aside. "You know we need this merger to go through. Everyone is making sacrifices, and I don't think I need to remind you that there is no alternative, because without this going through, Saint Luke's General will close."

Kathy knows that he is telling the truth but can't keep herself from complaining about how her nurses are being treated. "I know that, but it seems that my nurses are the ones hit hardest by the new memorandums. Most of them are taking benefit cuts and working more overtime when they'd prefer instead to see more nurses hired. I am afraid that if things continue like this, it will only be a matter of time before we are dealing with a strike or a mass exodus of the hospital's best health-care providers."

"I know it seems that way, but without the merger, no one has a job. Do the math. It's either work extra hours now or work no hours later. You choose!" Fed up with Kathy's tirade and lack of seeing the big picture, the chief walks off, leaving Kathy standing alone in the hall. She knows he is right but walks off irritated in the opposite direction anyway.

Back on the floor, Kathy continues to be bombarded all day with inquiries from staff members wanting to know what she's going to do about their unjust treatment. As the day progresses, so does Kathy's frustration, but she knows she can't let it show. The last thing she needs is to have her staff of nurses walk out. So unfortunately this means making reassurances to them she's not sure she can keep and trying desperately to hold her poise as best she can, all the while churning inside. The weight of this reality feels like a heavy burden on her shoulders.

Continuing her shift in the ER, Kathy's day goes from bad to worse. The first of the offenses comes when, in exam room eight, a four-year-old boy with the flu projectile vomits all over the front of her. This is followed a few hours later by a drunken sixty-year-old homeless man in exam room six, who smells of whiskey and fish, proceeding to urinate on her while sitting on the edge of the examining table as Kathy is cleaning a cut to his head. To top things off, at the end of her long day, she finds herself stranded alone in the bathroom, sitting in a stall that she didn't realize until it was too late is completely out of toilet paper. Exhausted and frustrated by the circumstances of her day, she exclaims as she looks up to the heavens, "Seriously!"

CHAPTER 8
GRANDKIDS

Franc

After the book-club ladies have received their drinks and bread, Franc heads to the back. Making her way through the kitchen toward her office where she takes a seat at her desk, she is followed by the pitter-patter of her mother's footsteps. "What is it, Mom?" she asks, not really wanting to know the answer.

"You know I'm not getting any younger. When are you going to give me some grandkids? You see how happy your sisters are with their little ones running around. Maybe it's time for you to find some nice man and settle down," suggests her mother.

Looking up from her laptop, she replies in her usual dismissive tone, "Mom, get over it."

"I'm just saying your eggs aren't getting any younger, you know? But don't worry. I heard that Susan Sarandon lady had a baby at forty-five," states Mom.

With the timing of a saint, Derek pops into the office and interrupts her mom's lecture. Looking relieved at the intrusion, Franc asks without hesitation, "Perfect timing. What can I do for you?"

Giving the floor to Derek, standing in the doorway, Sophia looks back at Franc and whispers before heading back to the dining room, "Just remember what I said."

"Oh, don't worry. If I do forget, I am sure you'll remind me later," she answers with sarcasm.

Ignoring the awkward conversation between Sophia and Franc, Derek says, "Well, I thought you would like to know a Mr. Robinson at table four requested to speak to the chef. He said he would like to thank him for the wonderful meal tonight."

"Thanks for letting me know. I will be sure to have Roman stop by his table, and I will do the same when I get back on the floor." Then she awkwardly adds, "So, do you have plans this weekend?"

He lets the sound of her question linger in his ears as his pulse begins to race and his cheeks flush with heat. He has been waiting so long for Franc to lower her guard and give into their mutual feelings for each other. "No, not really. Why?" he asks hesitantly, not wanting to reveal the true depth of his excitement.

Second-guessing her inquiry, she begins to stutter. "Oh, um, nothing. I was just curious."

With a look of confusion and disappointment, he pauses before answering, "Okay, then." Letting out a sigh, he walks away weighted with frustration.

Shutting her computer, Franc can't help but feel embarrassed and annoyed at herself for letting her mom get to her again. She mumbles under her breath, "This is ridiculous. What are you doing?"

CHAPTER 9

STANLEY AND INDIGESTION

At the table, Ali begins to eat pieces of bread one after the other without pause. Watching as Ali inhales carb after carb, barely coming up for air, Diane gives her a look, no words, just a look. Seeing Diane's look of query as her hand reaches into the bread basket for another piece, Ali responds with a full mouth, "Gimme a break. I've been living on green smoothies for a month straight. This is my one day of free eating, and I plan to take full advantage of it."

Putting her hands up in the air as a sign of surrender, Diane replies, "Hey, no judgment here. I know I speak for all of us when I say I just hope that bread defuses the gas fermenting in your bowels."

⇥ ⇤

Ali's and **Good Morning New York**

The display on the alarm clock sitting on the nightstand reads 3:40 a.m. Ali rolls out of bed carefully, trying not to disturb Princess Abigail, her cat, who is sprawled out on the pillow next to her. As she makes her way to the shower, Ali can hear the cat meowing in protest from her warm, cozy spot on the bed before stretching and getting down from her throne to follow Ali into the bathroom. Reaching down to comfort Princess Abigail, Ali scratches her head and agrees, "I know, I hate mornings too." Crossing the black-honed, slate, heated floors, Ali opens the glass shower door and reaches in to start the hot water. Today, like most mornings, Ali is walking through her morning ritual, barely opening her eyes. Despite the fact that she has been getting up at the same time for the past ten years, somehow her body still puts up a fight.

After her shower, Ali puts on her usual attire for the ride into the studio—a pair of old sweats bottoms and a matching UCLA hoodie. She knows her stylist will have her wardrobe waiting for her when she gets into work. So there is no need to wear anything else. As she makes her way to the kitchen, Princess Abigail circles Ali's legs and meows incessantly, making sure to let Ali know that she is ready for her breakfast.

"Yes, I know, Your Highness. You're hungry. I am getting your food ready as quickly as I can." Once the cat has been fed, Ali begins to make her own breakfast. It's been the same gagging healthy breakfast for the past four weeks. Every morning she has a green smoothie chock full of broccoli, kale, cucumber, and frozen bananas.

After filling the food processor, she puts the frozen bananas back in the freezer and pauses to put a bright-pink circle and smiley face on today's date on the New York City's firefighters' calendar that hangs on the fridge—book club! This joyful color is in clear contrast to the other days of the month, which are marked with large black *X*s.

Arriving at the studio at four forty-five with smoothie in hand, she is ready to go into the morning meeting and discuss what will be featured on today's episode of *Good Morning New York*. The small room is filled with other hosts and some of their interns. Ali takes her usual seat at the end of the table, farthest away from her temptation, the platter of deliciously sinful doughnuts. The show's producer and the bane of Ali's existence, Stanley, goes over the day's guests, hot topics, and relevant details. An hour later, the meeting comes to an end, and Stanley dismisses everyone, everyone, that is, except for Ali.

"Can you stay behind for a moment?" he asks. Leaning against the conference table next to where Ali is seated, Stanley crosses his arms and begins his conversation. "Listen, Ali, you know that you are America's sweetheart and you've been with us a long time, but with your contract coming up for renewal, you need to continue to earn your spot." He then goes on to inform her of more bad news. "The sponsors are concerned that the viewership is slipping. They feel they would like *Good Morning New York* to appeal to a more, how should I put it, um, youthful audience."

Responding defensively, Ali replies, "I know the numbers have been slipping, but I've done everything you have asked of me. This year alone, you've had me jumping out of planes and interviewing the latest teen sensation, and might I remind you about the segment where you had me slather bird shit on my face because it promised to be the latest miracle for erasing ten years off a woman's face. And, Stanley, I have done it all without complaint."

Knowing the gravity of her contract being up for renewal, she changes her tone from one of anger to one of confidence. She goes on to assure Stanley that he can count on her. Confidently she says she can and will bring in the numbers. After making her dramatic stand, Ali, full of bravado, begins to leave the room, carrying herself as if she were playing a role in a made-for-TV drama. But before she can escape with her dignity, Stanley reminds her of one more thing. "Oh, and remember the camera puts on ten pounds."

Walking out of the conference room and down the hall feeling angry and frustrated, Ali grumbles, "What the hell? Not only does he want me to be younger, but now I have to be thinner too. Great! It's not like I haven't been living on pureed rabbit food and slathering anti-aging cream on my face and neck every night. What else does he want me to do? You know I'm not Superman. I can't fly around the earth and turn back time. Ten pounds, what an arrogant prick!"

On her way to her dressing room, Ali passes her young, beautiful blond assistant/intern, Ashley, who innocently asks, "Is everything okay, Ali?"

Feeling vulnerable, Ali pauses and looks directly at her but gives no reply and then continues on her way to her dressing room, shutting the door behind her. Looking around the room, Ali sees earlier photos of herself from throughout her career, where she was interviewing heads of states, top political figures, and publishers. Acknowledging her past accomplishments, she mutters, "Shouldn't my track record speak for itself? The sponsors should feel grateful to have me." However, in her next breath, self-doubt begins to creep in. "Or are they right? Have I lost my appeal? Am I just fooling myself?"

Feeling the blow to her self-esteem and hoping for some reassurance, Ali calls her agent, Nicole Buckman, for some guidance and support.

Trying to be helpful but knowing the reality of today's television, Nicole tells Ali to stop trying to be a news reporter. She tells her that's not what *Good Morning New York* is about anymore. She also reminds Ali that she is an entertainer on a morning show. "So go out there, and find something to entertain them with." She suggests Ali try different, more "hip" stories.

Finding little comfort in what her agent had to say, Ali hangs up the phone and questions aloud, "Not a reporter...an 'entertainer'? And 'hip,' what the hell does that even mean?"

CHAPTER 10

DINNER SPECIALS

As Franc approaches the table to tell the ladies about tonight's dinner specials, she does it with caution, knowing one too many times in the past she has stepped up to that table to hear some of the most shocking revelations she has ever heard in her life. Remembering how hard it is to keep a straight face when you've just heard Kathy talk about how her husband, Ed, likes to role-play.

"Tonight's dinner specials are lobster fettuccini with a side of seasonal vegetables. We also have gnocchi in a pesto cream sauce with wild mushrooms, sundried tomatoes, and crispy pancetta," announces Franc.

Launching in to take the table's order, Franc starts with Kathy. "I will take the steak medium rare," she says.

"Do you want it with a side of red potatoes with tarragon or the polenta drizzled with truffle oil?" questions Franc.

"With the polenta, thanks," answers Kathy.

Melissa chimes in, "Yum, I'll have the same. I bought a bottle of truffle oil last week from Whole Foods and have been dying to try it out."

"I think you are really going to like it," Franc says confidently. Looking toward Ali, she continues, "And for you?"

"I think I will stick with the usual," Ali replies without hesitation.

Being familiar with Ali's order, Franc nods. "Three-cheese mac-n-cheese. Should I add crumbled bacon on top?"

"Now is that really a question?" quips Ali.

"Bacon it is." Smiling, Franc writes her order on her pad.

Next is Diane, who orders tonight's special of lobster fettuccini.

"Oh, that sounds delish. I will take the same," says Bette with a grin while she hands her menu back to Franc.

Lastly, Franc turns her attention toward Sarah, who says, "I think I'll try the eggplant Parmesan tonight."

After taking their orders, Franc refills the wineglasses for Diane, Kathy, Melissa, Ali, and Rita and then lets Sarah and Bette know she will be right back with their next drinks after she drops off their dinner orders in the kitchen. Franc then collects the remaining menus and heads off toward the kitchen.

CHAPTER 11

A WEDDING AND A FUNERAL

Kathy turns to Sarah. "You haven't told us how your sister's wedding went."

Grinning, Rita adds, "Yeah, tell us about your date. Did she put out?"

Diane replies to the question before Sarah has a chance to respond, saying, "Ha-ha, very funny. You know the only reason I was invited was because I did the floral arrangements. And besides, Sarah didn't have a plus one, and she didn't want to face her family alone. So I, being a good friend, said yes."

Bette continues questioning Sarah, "Tell us, how did the feuding parents do? I hope they didn't make too big a scene."

"No, surprisingly they were fine, and they let Beth be the focus of the night. Mom was there with her new husband, and Dad sat with my brother Matt. I think after seven years, they have finally figured out how to be civil to one another, at least in public anyway. I've got to say, though, I am not sure how my dad does it. I mean, if I found out my wife was having an affair with my business partner, I'm not so sure if I could ever be civil." She goes on to add, "There was, however, another couple that had a lot of heads at the reception turning."

"Who?" asks Ali.

"Well, Diane, would you like to tell them? Or should I call you Mom?" sassed Sarah.

"Wait a minute. What? No. Diane and your dad?" questions Ali, confused.

"Yep, they danced together all night. I even saw him whisper in her ear during one of the slow songs," tattles Sarah.

Cheeks flushed with embarrassment over the possibility of her new romance, Diane continues to sip her wine and giggle like a schoolgirl. "What can I say? Your dad is charming and funny. He made me laugh." Putting the rumors to rest, Diane continues, "Oh, it was all very innocent. He came over to compliment me on the floral arrangements, and then one thing led to another. The next thing I knew, we were on the dance floor. That's all."

Not one to mince words, Bette bluntly asks, "Is he a good kisser?"

Diane looks at Bette as if she were crazy. "Are you out of your mind? We didn't kiss. All we did was dance," she answers firmly.

Melissa, a sucker for romance, can't help but continue the questioning, saying, "So tell us, are you going to see him again?" She adds, "You never go out. I think this could be great."

"I go out," says Diane indignantly.

"Going out with your gay assistant doesn't count. She means going out on a real date," quips Rita.

With a soft motherly tone, Melissa agrees, saying, "Honey, I think you're ready to get back out there. It's been such a long time, and I think Phil would want you to be happy."

But before Diane can respond, Sarah interjects, "I hope so. I have been telling her for years that I think the two of them would make a great couple."

Smiling back at Sarah, Diane replies, "I know you have, sweetie." She continues, "Well, as a matter of fact, yes, we are having lunch on Saturday. I'll let you know how things go."

Diane and Good-Bye

It is a cold October Saturday morning when Diane's husband, Phil, complains as he gets out of bed, rubbing his chest, "I don't think I should've been helping myself to your plate of jalapeño-stuffed chicken last night, but I couldn't help myself." Continuing to rub his chest, he adds, "It looked so good when the waiter brought it over to you."

"Yeah, well, you know you're going to be paying for that indulgence all day." Diane adds, "Phil, you know how spicy food gives you heartburn."

"I know, but it tastes so good," Phil replies with a sheepish grin on his face as he walks to the bathroom wearing blue boxers printed with red anchors and a white undershirt.

As she watches her six-foot-two-inch, graying husband make his way to the bathroom rubbing his chest, she can't help but grin as she imagines what he might have been like as a small boy. No matter how old they get or how long they've been married, Phil, like most men, turns into a helpless toddler when he doesn't feel well. Trying to help him with his discomfort, she tells him, "There are antacids in the medicine cabinet, next to the Band-Aids." As she puts on her cozy red terry-cloth robe that lies on the leather bench at the foot of their bed, Diane shouts to Phil, who's now in the bathroom, "I am going to go down and start the coffee."

On her way, Diane pauses to pet the head of her beloved aging dog lying on the navy-and-white-striped rug in front of the fireplace in the sitting room, which is adjacent to the kitchen. "Good morning, Molly." Happy to receive the attention, Molly stretches and yawns before slowly making her way to stand. "Come on, old girl," Diane says. "It's time to go out and do your morning duties."

As Diane opens the back door, the cold wind whips through the room. Feeling the cold air, Molly is reluctant to leave the warmth and needs to be gently coaxed outside. Looking down at the dog, Diane begins to lecture her, saying, "Fine, I'll go with you, but I am warning you, I don't plan to keep doing this every morning. You're going to need to put on your big-girl pants and start going out alone again." Looking back outside to the cold autumn morning, she continues her stance, "Especially when it starts to snow." Giving Molly a gentle rub on her head, Diane gives her orders as she steps outside: "Now come on. Let's make this quick."

A few moments later, Diane is back in her kitchen, scooping heaping tablespoons of coffee into the coffeemaker and praying for it to brew at lightning speed. Her little morning excursion to the backyard has left her freezing.

Coming into the kitchen, Phil walks over to Diane and greets her with a kiss on the top of her head. "Good morning, beautiful." Feeling the warmth of her freshly showered husband, Diane turns to embrace him. "So I see Molly made you go out with her again this morning," he says as she grips him tightly.

"What, can't a wife hug her handsome husband without having a reason?" protests Diane.

"Sure, but your bone-chilling hands give you away," says Phil, laughing as he feels Diane's hands go under his shirt.

"Well, sometimes she needs company with her in order for her to go out," explains Diane.

"You spoil her. You know that, right?" he asks her affectionately.

"Yeah, I know, but look at her. How can you look in those big brown eyes and tell her no?" Diane says as she bends over and scratches under Molly's chin.

The dripping has stopped, and the heavenly scent of freshly brewed coffee fills the kitchen. Diane pours herself a cup and begins to fill one for Phil.

Stopping her before she can finish filling his cup, Phil says, "No, thanks, I'm still not feeling well. I think I'll wait."

"Okay, but you don't know what you are missing," says Diane as she closes her eyes to take her first sip. "I was going to make some oatmeal. Do you want me to make you a bowl?"

Not feeling up for breakfast either, Phil replies, "Nah, I'll just grab something later while I'm at the clubhouse."

"Oh, that's right. Sorry, I've been so caught up at the shop getting ready for the Millers' wedding next week that I forgot you are playing golf this morning with Jared. What do you say we plan to stay in tonight and catch up? We've both been so busy at work. We can open a nice bottle of wine and snuggle up on the sofa to watch a movie. What do you think?" asks Diane.

"A night in sounds great," answers Phil as he grabs his keys from the counter, kisses her on the cheek, and heads out the door.

After Phil leaves, Diane takes her coffee into the sitting room, with Molly following slowly behind. She turns on her laptop to answer e-mails from a file folder in the inbox labeled "Millers' Wedding." Once she opens the file, Diane begins to frantically go through any new e-mails and then picks up her phone to start on the long list of people she needs to call. For most people, Christmas is the big gift-giving occasion, but that's not the case for Diane and Phil. They've always felt Christmas should be focused more on family and friends and that birthdays were the days to really celebrate with lavish gifts and parties. This year is no exception. Diane has been planning a surprise party for Phil's fifty-ninth birthday for weeks and has hidden all the details in the "Millers' Wedding" file. Her first call is to Kathy. She states, "The coast is clear," when she hears Kathy answer.

"He still doesn't suspect a thing?" questions Kathy.

"Nothing, he thinks he is just going out for a round of golf with a friend from the office."

Kathy is quick to compliment her on her deceptive planning skills: "Smart thinking to enlist Jared. He will keep Phil busy for hours."

"I know. It's great. Jared said he told Phil their tee time is at ten, but it's really not until ten forty-five, so he could buy us a little more time."

"Brilliant," says Kathy, laughing.

"I figure that means we have a good four hours before he finishes playing. That is unless Jared can come up with more distractions," says Diane with enthusiasm.

"Great! So what time are the other ladies going to get there?" asks Kathy, talking about the other members of the book club.

"They all said they should be here by noon to help set things up and decorate," answers Diane happily.

"Perfect, I will see you then," says Kathy before hanging up.

⟞⟝

It's after five in the evening when Diane returns home. Per her request, the house is empty of life other than Molly, who has been sleeping on Diane's bed waiting for her to come home. The birthday decorations and food have all been taken away by friends, and a stockpot of homemade chicken soup has been left in her refrigerator in hopes that Diane will muster the energy to eat something.

As Diane walks aimlessly through her home, she begins to feel like the walls are closing in and suffocating her. With frantic determination, she grabs Molly's leash and leaves. Confused and heartbroken, she finds herself wandering the streets, finally ending up at a neighboring elementary school miles from her home. There she takes a rest on the middle seat of the swing set and begins to cry. She doesn't just cry; she breaks, the kind of breaking that only happens as a result of complete and utter tragedy. Cursing, shouting, and crying to God, herself, or whoever will listen, she asks, "Why? Why Phil? Heart attack, he's only fifty-nine. He's a good man. He's my man. I need him." Looking to heaven, she says, "He's mine. You can't have him. Give him back." Pleading with every fiber of her body and soul, she says, "Please, God, give him back. I never got the chance to say good-bye or tell him that I love him one last time." In a hushed tone, she begs to the one who holds her universe, "Oh God, please. Please, tell him that I love him." Exhausted and cold from the hours spent wandering the streets, Diane returns home to the comfort of her bedroom and the memories of her life with Phil.

Trying to respect their friend's request for privacy, the book-club ladies give Diane her space. However, as the night progresses, one by one they each flock to her home, knowing at some point Diane might emerge from her bedroom and want a hand to hold or arms to fall into, and they want to be there waiting for her whenever that need occurs.

Bette is the first to arrive. Stepping up to the door, she isn't sure what to do. Should she knock, ring the doorbell, what? To her relief, she finds the door is unlocked and lets herself inside. The home is dark and silent. She is greeted by Molly but only for a moment before she, too, retreats to the bedroom. Throughout the next few hours, each of the friends arrives to give her comfort, love, and support. Over the next three weeks, the friends stay by Diane's side, helping to make funeral arrangements and financial decisions. They take shifts throughout the day and night making sure Diane never feels alone. This act of friendship, love, and sisterhood is something Diane will remember and reflect on for the rest of her life. It is a bond that can never be broken.

CHAPTER 12

RELEVANCE AND MOTHERHOOD

Getting things back on track, Rita asks, "All right, back to the wedding. Did Beth make you wear a tiara and dress made of pink taffeta with bows?"

"Worse! It was a plum floor-length organza gown with white opera gloves. Oh, and because I was the maid of honor, I had the pleasure of wearing a large white bird attached to a headband so I would stand out among the other girls in the wedding party."

Rita is barely able to speak through her laughter. "Well, I bet you did stand out!"

"Ha-ha, very funny. Do you know Beth actually had the audacity to tell me that she thinks I should wear the headband the next time I go out with my friends? Yeah, she thinks it would make a beautiful accessory and catch a lot of gentlemen's attention. I didn't have the heart to tell her that is not the kind of attention I am looking for. Furthermore, anyone who might be attracted to a woman wearing a bird on her head is not the kind of guy I'd be interested in."

Bette takes this opportunity to ask Melissa about the New Jersey Mafia housewife–inspired outfit she is wearing tonight. "That is some outfit, Melissa. Where did you get it?"

Completely flattered by Bette's inquiry, Melissa proudly answers, "Aw, thanks, Bette. I got it at Forever 21."

Melissa Trends, Fashion, and Family

It's spring break, and Rachael, Melissa's daughter, is having a few girls over to stay the night. As Melissa gets closer to her daughter's room, she can hear music blaring as well as the friends talking and laughing. The cheerful sounds make Melissa smile with joy. Armed with a plateful of homemade salted-caramel brownies, Melissa knocks on her daughter's bedroom door in hopes she'll be invited in to hang with the girls. She prides herself on being one of the "cool" moms, the kind of mom who stays in touch with fashion, music, and trends. However, to her disappointment, as she enters the room, Rachael suddenly goes quiet. This, however, doesn't faze the two friends, Cari and Megan. They love it when Melissa joins them. In fact, on many occasions both Cari and Megan have told Rachael how much they wish their own moms were more like Melissa...

"Rachael, your mom is so cool, and I love the way she dresses. All my mom ever wears is yoga pants and a running jacket. And she doesn't even run. I think she wears them because of the elastic waistband," Cari once said, giggling.

Megan has said many times before, "You are so lucky that your mom likes the same music as you. You and your mom can go to concerts together. My mom always tells me to turn my music down whenever she passes my room."

Ignoring her daughter's quiet demeanor, Melissa takes a seat at the end of Rachael's bed. Immediately, Cari comments to Melissa that she has the same top as Melissa has on, only that hers is in blue. With that friendly observation, Melissa dives in with the latest dish with the girls, disregarding the look of embarrassment plastered on Rachael's face.

"So, Meg, how was your date with Scott last week?" Melissa asks. "And, Cari, what's going on with the job hunt? Did you have any luck getting the sales position at Hollister? Do you want me to put in a good word for you next time I am at the mall?"

After filling up with an earful from the friends, Melissa sneaks back down the hall to her room and quietly climbs back into bed. Carefully, she pulls her teal comforter up to her shoulders, trying not to wake Ryan. Pleased with herself for being so stealthy, she lays her head on her pillow and grins just seconds before she is startled when Ryan utters, "Go ahead. Tell me the latest." Thrilled that he wants to hear all about what she has just learned, she sits up in bed, turns on the crystal lamp sitting next to her on her nightstand, and begins telling Ryan what she has just been privy to.

The next morning the girls spend their time primping and eating multiple bowls of cereal in front of the television before leaving to go hang out at Megan's house. Watching as Rachael and her friends leave, Melissa waits for the door to close before heading straight for the home office down the hall from the kitchen. There she reaches for the laptop sitting on top of a large Hendrix desk she bought last spring from Pottery Barn. Coffee in hand, she's ready for another morning of gathering trending topics and, most importantly, fashion advice by visiting the E! and Style networks, YouTube, and Pinterest posts, anything to get to the latest dos and don'ts—this, along with a healthy dose of the latest celebrity gossip. Melissa takes detailed notes on her phone that she will use later that afternoon on her weekly excursion to the mall.

Once showered, Melissa spends a considerable amount of time in her walk-in closet, hoping to put together the perfect outfit for her day of shopping. Pleased with her choice of four-inch ankle boots, a pink infinity scarf, and fuchsia skinny jeans, she confidently heads out the door to the cab waiting to take her to the Manhattan Mall on Broadway at Thirty-Third Street.

A short twenty-minute drive later, she arrives at her destination, the holy grail of teenage fashion, Forever 21. There, she is greeted by name by the young salesgirls. As usual, she is fawned over by the staff, who knows that with the right influence Melissa never leaves the store empty-handed. As quickly as they can, the team of Kardashian look-alikes confine Melissa to a fitting room and begin their dance of persuasion, showing her their newest arrivals and the season's top must-haves. Hoping to add to the final total, the salesgirls provide Melissa with an assortment of accessory pieces and shoes to finish off each ensemble. To her face, these real-life mean girls are all smiles and kindness. However, unbeknown to her, behind her back they snicker.

"I would be so embarrassed if my mom ever dressed like that."

"I know, right? Like, how old is she, forty?"

"Right? She looks ridiculous."

Later that afternoon, Melissa is back at the apartment, pacing by the front window, hoping to see the mailman. When she finally does see him, she squeals with delight. She knows he brings what she has been waiting for all month. "Ahh! The latest edition of *Seventeen* magazine has arrived!" She takes the elevator down to the lobby, where she greets the mailman and pulls the waiting magazine out of his hands, leaving the rest of the mail for him to put in their mailbox. Handling the magazine with all the care of a mother holding her own newborn baby, Melissa, too impatient to wait for the elevator, decides to run to the stairs and climb the three flights to her apartment. Opening the door, she enters, out of breath from her unexpected morning workout but excited to begin her studies. The mailman was late today, so she knows that she has only limited time to riffle through the magazine before her daughter gets back home.

Melissa meticulously opens the plastic surrounding the magazine. Being ever so careful not to rip, tear, or wrinkle the pages or—God forbid—the cover, she uses her cell phone to take pictures of the fashion dos-and-don'ts images. Only after thoroughly going over each page does she reseal the plastic cover on the magazine with the precision and care of a heart surgeon. She then returns the magazine to their mailbox to join the other letters waiting in the lobby. Noticing the clock in the lobby, she realizes how late it is, and she hurries over to the elevator. Once inside, she begins tapping her manicured nails on the handrail in efforts to quicken the trip back to the apartment because tonight is her date night with Ryan, and she is eager to try out one of the new fashion dos she picked up earlier that day.

Meanwhile, across town her husband is trying hard to finish up his work at the office so he can meet Melissa at their favorite bistro, the Green Frog. It's a small French bistro they found one night a few years back as they were walking along the High Line, a park near Tenth and Thirtieth. Putting the final touches on a blueprint for a project he is working on in Brooklyn, Ryan shuts his computer and leaves his office for the evening.

He arrives at the bistro a little early, so he takes a seat in the quaint bar adjacent to the entry while he waits for Melissa to arrive. Enjoying a tall, cold pint of local ESB, he reminisces about the outfits his wife has come up with over the years. He never quite knows what she will look like when she arrives somewhere. From her hairstyles to fashion trends, she does keep things interesting, to say the least. He remembers the time when she showed up to his architectural firm's Christmas party with the ends of her hair dyed bright pink because it was all the rage. Shaking his head, he thinks to himself, "She's already so beautiful. She doesn't need to be the trendiest person in the room to be interesting to me or our daughter. She's perfect just the way she is."

However, he understands why she has such deep-rooted insecurities. The stories that Melissa has shared with him about her childhood are nothing short of child abuse. Far too many times, Melissa had to deal with her alcoholic mother letting her down. How many days did Melissa have to come home after school to a dark house, not knowing if she would see her mom passed out on the sofa or in the bedroom with a man? Then there were the all-too-frequent times when her mother would leave on a bender and not come home for days. Thankfully, Melissa was bright, and despite the uncertainties of her home life, she did remarkably well in school and was able to keep what was happening behind closed doors secret from her friends and teachers.

He also understands her desire to fit in. He can only imagine how hard it was for Melissa to keep up her deception, to wear the right clothes, to watch the right television shows, or to listen to the current songs on the radio. All of these were skills honed to fool the others around her, to make them think she was a normal child with a normal home. When it came time for parent-teacher conferences, Melissa made excuses for why her mom would cancel at the last minute. She usually used the cover "Sorry, my mom got called to an out-of-town work conference last minute and is very sorry that she won't be able to make it tonight. So she sent me instead. If you give me the papers, I can bring them home and have her sign them." It astonishes Ryan that no one at the school ever caught on.

Over the years, he has come to admire and understand the depths to which Melissa will go to not make the same mistakes her mother made and to stay involved in Rachael's life. Her willingness and desire to find things in common and her struggles to try to remain relevant in their seventeen-year-old daughter's life are feats to be commended. From the years of volunteering every chance she could get at Rachael's school to staying up to speed on the latest fads and crazes, Melissa does it all. His train of thought is suddenly broken when he sees Melissa being escorted to the bar wearing a simple winter-white dress and nude pumps. She looks radiant.

Once seated at their table, they order a bottle of merlot and an appetizer. It is one of Melissa's favorites, *cassoulet au canard* (baked white-bean and duck casserole). The very thought of it makes Melissa beam with anticipation. Ryan can't help but smile. He loves the way Melissa lights up when she talks about food. He knows her passion for food is second only to the love she has for their family.

CHAPTER 13

DIANE AND THE SECRETS OF HIGH SOCIETY

After Bette's comment about Melissa's "twenty-something" outfit, Sarah turns the attention to Bette. Looking her up and down, Sarah says with a straight face, "Well, my friend, that certainly is a statement you're projecting tonight. I haven't seen a getup like that since the last time I watched reruns of *Leave It to Beaver.*"

Bette raises her right hand to her necklace, gingerly strokes her strand of pearls, and replies with attitude, "Well, I think they are divine."

On the other side of the table, Diane looks over the top of her wineglass and notices a couple walking into the restaurant and suddenly chokes on her sip of wine. Kathy looks at Diane and asks if she is okay. Diane responds with a nod but looks red-cheeked and flustered.

After turning toward the entrance to see what all the fuss is about, Ali asks Diane with an eager tone, "Okay, what do you know about them? I just had Governor Mitchell and his wife on my show. They seemed so normal." Knowing a juicy story is about to ensue, she then adds, "Details! Don't leave anything out."

As with most of the who's who in New York, Diane has the dish on the couple, and she's all too overjoyed to share the news with her friends at the table. First looking around the restaurant to make sure no one can hear what she is about to say, Diane leans forward and in a hushed tone tells them—with the addition of air quotes to emphasize her point—"Well, I know for a fact that this 'happily' married governor isn't so 'happily' married. How, you might ask, do I know this? Well, let me tell you." She pauses, taunting her friends. "Because every Monday for the past five months, he has had two dozen red roses delivered to an apartment on the Upper East Side. And his wife doesn't live on the Upper East Side, if you know what I mean." Then she sits back in the booth, raises her left eyebrow, and takes a sip of wine. Diane is notorious for her ability to raise one eyebrow to great effect! She then watches in delight as the ladies all gasp at the news she has just delivered.

Melissa, looking at Diane in awe, tells her, "You know everything about everyone. You are so frickin' cool," a statement that brings the rest of them to chuckles.

"Well, you wouldn't believe what people will do and say when they think only the help is around," replies Diane.

⇌ ⇋

Diane and the "Help"

Arriving in two white work vans with the Petals logo prominently displayed on either side, Diane and her crew of four assistants pull up at their destination. It is a gorgeous quintessential East Hampton home overlooking the water, complete with weathered-cedar shingle siding and a large white wraparound porch that leads to the manicured lawn with a large rectangular swimming pool. The pool is surrounded by woven lounge chairs topped with blue-and-white-striped cushions with matching umbrellas dotted throughout the area. A pair of eight-foot-tall spiral topiaries marks the entrance to the pool area. Like most of the homes in the area, it is just steps away from the beach and the crashing roar of the ocean waves.

Diane is dressed in her company's uniform, consisting of khaki pants and a white oxford shirt with her company's logo, "Petals," written in green over the left pocket. For a little pop of color, Diane added a coral scarf around her neck to match her alligator penny loafers. And for her own amusement, Diane is also wearing a hot-pink bra and panties in leopard print. Her feelings are the uniform and scarf are for the clients, but the undergarments are for her. She relishes the thought of wearing something garish and wild to offset the pristine environments of most of her clients.

Today, she and her assistants are at the home of Audrey and Ben Sheppardson for a posh baby shower.

Per the request of Audrey, the mother-to-be, all the flowers are yellow, as to not give away the sex of the baby until the couple is ready to do the big reveal later that evening. It's three in the afternoon, and the guests won't be arriving until seven. So there's plenty of time for Diane and her crew to set the floral arrangements and leave before any guests arrive. Once the flowers are set on the designated tables in the home, they can now concentrate on the area by the pool, where most of the baby shower will take place. Diane assigns each of her assistants an area to focus on.

"Lisa, work on the open bar. Use the small arrangements there. That way the bartender has more room for the champagne flutes. Kris, you can work on the dining tables, and, Shawn, please start placing the larger arrangements on the buffet tables. Cindy, you are going to be in charge of the gift and dessert tables."

An hour later, Diane pauses at the patio door, which overlooks the beautifully landscaped lawn. There she can observe the progress her assistants have made thus far. Each arrangement must look perfect from this vantage point, because this will be the first thing the guests see when making their way to the elegant backyard baby shower.

Going back to one of the vans to retrieve a vase of lilies, Diane sees the mom-to-be in a heated discussion with her brother-in-law. Not one to turn away from a possible piece of interesting gossip, Diane tries to be as quiet as she can while making her way to the open side door of the van. There, she climbs in and moves to the vacant floor space in the center area between the two front seats. Peering through the flowers, she positions herself to get a better view of the two arguing. Having purposefully left the sliding door of the van open, Diane can hear the whole argument that is unfolding right in front of her. To her surprise, she hears Audrey tell the brother-in-law that she has no intention of telling her husband of their one-night stand. Diane lets out a sound of astonishment when, in reply, she hears the brother-in-law insist that Audrey get a paternity test.

Startled by what sounds like a loud gasp, the couple stops and turns in the direction of the van. Diane immediately drops silently to the floor of the van, just in the nick of time. Lying there, she can't believe what she is hearing and thinks to herself: "I can't wait to get back to the store and tell Chad. He's going to be so mad he missed this!" Diane lies there on the floor for what feels like hours, silently praying that the "once-lovers" squabble continues and hoping that her eavesdropping isn't discovered.

She giggles to herself and talks quietly aloud to her deceased husband, saying, "Phil, are you hearing this? All those times you wondered why I like my job so much, well…" Filled with the juicy gossip and no longer hearing voices quarreling, Diane gives in to the overwhelming leg cramp that is steadily moving from her calf to the insole of her right foot. Quietly groaning from the pain, she stretches slowly upward to see if the "couple" is still out there. However, to her dismay it looks as though the two have already parted ways. Resigned that there is nothing more to hear, she climbs out of the van and brushes away any loose flower petals from her hair and clothes. Collecting the vase of flowers she had initially come out for, Diane makes her way back to the house. Taking good measure to act as normal as possible, she nevertheless looks around to see if the two have taken their spat somewhere else. When she comes up empty on her search for the squabbling couple, Diane concedes her defeat and resumes her duties of decorating for the party.

CHAPTER 14

PORK AND WATERMELONS

Ali, like the others at the table, is not disappointed by Diane's piece of information. As promised, Diane's revelation about the governor leaves them all fuming, and one by one they begin shooting looks of disgust and contempt to the unaware man. It is Ali who is quick to point out how clear it is to her that his new young thing, whom he keeps in comfort on the side, must not be interested in his looks.

As Bette so beautifully describes him, "He looks like a troll."

"Well," comments Rita, "that troll has a lot of power, and to a lot of women in this town that *is* very attractive."

Melissa gives a little involuntary shudder. "I'm sorry, but it would take a lot more power and clout than that man's got for me to sleep with him; his gargantuan sweaty body climbing on top of you and beady little eyes. And don't get me started on his nipple-hugging slacks, ew!"

"Gross," says Sarah, laughing.

"That's nothing," says Rita. "You want to hear something really gross? Let's just say I have the pleasure of watching Jim and my two wonderful sons scratch their balls every morning as they stumble into the kitchen; now that's gross. I don't get it. I mean, what are they digging for? It's like they need to scratch themselves in order to wake up. Apparently, just like we women need a cup of coffee to get us revved up for our day, men, on the other hand, need a good ten-minute nut scratch to do the same."

Kathy jumps in with a tone of sweet sarcasm. "Who knew there was a scientific explanation for this morning ritual? That makes the act of watching Ed dig for gold in his boxers before opening the refrigerator each morning make a lot more sense. Thanks, Rita."

Rita quickly quips, "No problem. I'll let you know the next time I come up with any more words of wisdom to explain the lesser of the two sexes."

Melissa, adding fuel to the fire, says, "Well, I can let you in on another little unexpected treat I recently discovered about men. It's a little something I found while changing our sheets. Has anyone else noticed the crime scene left behind on the mattress pad where your husband sleeps? I was doing the laundry the other day and pulled off the sheets to throw them in the wash, and what I saw made me quake. I literally shuddered. It was a perfect imprint in mustard yellow of Ryan. It looked like one of those outlines police draw of some dead body they found in an alley."

Ali chimes in, "Seriously, men are pigs. Maybe being single isn't so bad. Listening to you ladies, I can't help but wonder how they're the same species as us. I mean, even if we all did start out the same, it's clear their species has evolved into some distorted strand of a low-hygiene, highly grotesque crossbreed. Who knows where things first started to go wrong? When did the mutation begin?"

Rita is quick to answer. "Take it from me, someone who's outnumbered three to one. I ask myself the same question on a daily basis."

Kathy raises both her eyebrows, mimicking Groucho Marx, and states, "Sure, men are pigs, but I wouldn't want to go my whole life on a diet without pork!"

This declaration is met with raised glasses. "I'll drink to that," says Sarah. The ladies then clink their glasses together in a united sisterhood.

Ali stops abruptly after the toast, in midair. She then sniffs the air and comments to the ladies that she swears she smells watermelon. Ali continues looking around the room, trying to figure out where the smell is coming from. Bringing her attention back to the table and her rumbling stomach, she takes a bite of a dinner roll. However, not feeling satisfied, Ali complains, "Our dinner is taking forever tonight." Taking another bite, she adds, "I haven't had solid food in so long I thought I had forgotten how to chew."

Rita smiles and assures her friend that dinner will be coming soon.

Trying to combat Ali's low-blood-sugar tantrum, Melissa picks up the bread basket and puts it in Ali's face, smiles, and says, "Do us all a favor and have another piece of bread."

Ali, sniffing the air, again asks, "Seriously, does anyone else smell watermelon?" Thinking of the last time she took a bite out of a big ripe watermelon, she adds, "Ah, fruit, sweet, juicy fruit."

Sarah, looking guilty, blurts out, "No," and then suspiciously starts looking around the room. Picking up the drink menu left behind by Franc, she methodically studies it from front to back. Trying desperately to change the subject, she announces, "Maybe I will try something different tonight," while uncrossing and recrossing her legs in the opposite direction under the table.

Ali continues her obsession. "There it is again. I swear I smell watermelon." She pauses to sniff the air. "Come on. Don't any of you smell that?" she asks.

Giving in to curiosity, Bette sniffs the air too. "Hey, so do I." Bette then makes a scene, sniffing around the table from left to right, circling the table. To Sarah's alarm, Bette stops when she reaches her and exclaims in an accusatory tone, "It's you. You smell like watermelons. Are you wearing watermelon lip gloss? What are you, twelve?"

Embarrassed, Sarah looks down toward the table to avoid eye contact with the ladies and sheepishly responds, "No, I'm not wearing watermelon lip gloss."

⟞⊹⊹⟝

Sarah and the Ad

Getting off the elevator on the ninth floor, Sarah greets her secretary, Mary, on her way to her office, room 915. It's an office located halfway down the hall, with floor-to-ceiling windows facing east. This allows the morning sun peeking through the tall concrete buildings opposite the street to cast soft hues of yellow around her space and dance across her desk, something that brings a smile to Sarah's face each morning. Mary informs Sarah that the package she has been waiting for has arrived and that she left it for her on her desk. Walking into her office, Sarah sees the package sitting just where Mary said it would be. Crossing the room, Sarah goes to her desk, but before she sits, she places her black leather bag next to her desk and hangs her trench coat neatly on the wooden rack in the corner before returning to address the waiting box.

Taking a seat at her desk, she opens her top drawer and pulls out a pair of scissors to carefully open the package. "Let's see what we have here." She wonders, "I don't see what all the fuss was about. Why did the VP, Kevin Bluntly, want me for this account? He knows I already have things I am working on with deadlines coming up in the next few weeks. He really should have given this account to Patrick."

Before she can finish that thought, she opens the box and looks inside. Stunned by what she sees, Sarah looks up from the box. She can't believe what's staring back at her. "Are you fucking kidding me?" To Sarah's disbelief, it's a box full of fruit-scented tampons in an array of neon colors. Questioning out loud to herself, she asks, "Who would invent such a thing? And how the hell am I supposed to come up with a slogan and ad campaign to sell it?"

When the initial shock of the absurdity of the product begins to wear off, Sarah tries to rise to the occasion, spouting self-affirmation and words of encouragement. "Okay, pull it together, and focus. You are good at your job. You can sell anything." She begins tossing around a few ideas. "What about…fresh as the farmers' market…or…forbidden fruit?" Chuckling, she says, "Gag!"

Discouraged, she goes on, saying, "Ugh, nothing sounds right. How could it? I mean, what can you say about fruit-scented tampons other than an ignorant man must have come up with it because a woman would never be so vulgar? Really, what woman in her right mind wants to have her vagina permeated with scented fruit while she's hemorrhaging buckets of O positive? And look at these colors." Pausing, she feels a flash of panic come across her. "Oh shit, what if they glow in the dark? Great! Now there's an image that's going to take a lot of wine to erase from my head!"

After coming up blank for ideas, her feelings of anger toward her VP continue to swell inside her. "Guess now I know why he gave me the product instead of

Patrick. I bet the two of them are having a big laugh at my expense right about now."

Sarah decides to put the box of vagina air fresheners aside and continue to work on her other accounts, knowing she can go back to it later, after she's had time to clear her head. While working diligently on the other accounts over the next few hours, Sarah continues to be distracted by the "box of candy for your hoo-ha." Despite her attempts to ignore the carton of disgust, Sarah can still see it out of the corner of her eye. It sits there on the shelf to the right of her desk, rudely mocking her. So with one swift motion, she opens the large bottom right-side drawer of her desk, drops the box inside, and slams the drawer shut. "Good riddance."

Midafternoon Sarah decides to take a much-needed break from her work and joins her friend Carol for a quick lunch at the deli on the bottom floor of their building. Trying to forget the inappropriate product waiting for her in her bottom drawer, Sarah decides not to reference it when Carol innocently asks what new ad she is working on. Instead, Sarah responds with a generic, "Oh, nothing special really. You know, same old stuff." Eager to change the subject, Sarah deflects the conversation away from her and onto Carol. "How about you? How are things in accounting?"

After filling up on a ham-and-cheese sandwich, two chocolate-chip cookies, and a large cup of ice tea to wash it all down, Sarah feels refreshed and ready to return to her office and face the box of dreaded horror. In spite of her self-motivational thoughts of encouragement, as she gets off the elevator and heads down the hall to her office, Sarah can feel the good energy and positive attitude diminishing with each step. The closer she gets to her office, the more it feels as if the absorbent cotton from the tampons is sucking the very life from her body.

Hours drag on, and still none of the slogans she is coming up with seem right for the ad campaign. Frustrated with her writer's block and out of sheer desperation, Sarah reluctantly decides to try the product out for herself. The irony of today's special account is not lost on Sarah. "Well, at least I am having my period. Maybe if I try one of these ludicrous things, an idea will come to me through osmosis." Embarrassed by the thought of someone seeing her on the way to the ladies' room with her little box of goodies, Sarah pulls out a file folder from her desk to conceal the unmentionable while she makes her way down the hall to the bathroom. Once inside the ladies' room, Sarah looks around and is relieved to see that it is empty. Purposefully, she chooses the last stall on the right and bravely enters. As she sits on the toilet, with her pencil skirt and panties down by her stilettos and the package perched on her lap, Sarah cautiously opens the box. Looking inside, she is again appalled by the vibrant neon colors. Reaching into the box with two fingers, she pulls out a watermelon-scented tampon. Justifying her decision, she tells herself, "At least it's pink, and as everyone knows, pink is the least offensive of the neon colors." Unwrapping the tampon, Sarah rolls her eyes as she smells the aggressive, overpowering watermelon scent that is now wafting through the bathroom and enveloping everything in its path. Wincing, she cautiously inserts it. Despite washing her hands several times after the deed was done, she sniffs her hands and can still smell the gagging, sweet scent of watermelon emanating from them. "Ugh!"

Walking nervously back toward her office, Sarah sees Mary stop typing and look up from her computer with a confused look on her face as Sarah approaches. Mortified, Sarah thinks to herself, "Oh crap! What if she can smell the decaying watermelon that now calls my vagina home?" Embarrassed, Sarah does not say a thing to Mary but instead picks up her pace and walks quickly by, careful not to make eye contact. Once past the reception desk and nearing her office, Sarah looks back over her shoulder and observes Mary sniffing the air again, pausing before resuming her typing.

CHAPTER 15

THE CONFESSION

Bette, still being a little pushy about the fruity aroma at the table, asks Sarah, "If it's not lip gloss, then what is it?" Continuing with a smug look on her face, she boldly states, "Oh, wait. I know what it is. It's edible underwear." Hearing this makes Melissa, Rita, Kathy, and Ali roll their eyes and make groans of disgust. Despite the disapproving tones around the table, Bette continues to prod. "You have a date later. Don't you? Don't you? I'm right, aren't I?"

Sarah answers, "No, I do not have a date later." Resigned to the fact that Bette will not let this go, she has but one option to stop the interrogation, and that is to tell the ladies about her day. Looking completely humiliated, she takes a deep breath and begins. "Well, my friends, I am trying out a new product that my firm has, and I'm supposed to come up with the slogan and ad campaign."

"For what, body lotion?" asks Rita.

Sarah answers, "I wish, but no." Blushing, she whispers, "It's a feminine product."

Intrigued, "Is it a scented lubricant?" inquires Melissa while silently considering the pros and cons of using such a product.

"No, it's not that either. Although I think that would be a whole lot easier than this," complains Sarah.

Kathy jokingly asks, "Like what, scented pads?"

Sarah, taking a deep breath, quickly and quietly replies, "You're close. It's fruit-scented tampons."

"What?" shouts Melissa.

Flabbergasted, Bette asks, "Are you kidding me?"

Sarah tries to quiet the ladies but to no avail. They are hysterical with laughter.

Melissa continues, "Fruit-scented tampons. That is so gross!"

"What idiot came up with that?" says Diane, laughing.

Ali and Rita look at each other and answer in unison, "A man."

"I was just kidding when I said pads." Kathy continues laughing so hard that she just about pees her pants. "Move it, ladies!" she shouts as she pushes Rita, Ali, and Bette out of the way, shoving herself to freedom. Relieving herself from the confinement of the booth, Kathy does her best impression of an Olympic speed walker, making a beeline to the bathroom. The friends in the booth can still hear her giggling as Kathy makes her way across the restaurant.

⊨ ⊨

CHAPTER 16

SOPHIA AND ROMAN WORKING TOGETHER

Back in the kitchen, Franc oversees the food prep and makes sure each plate leaving the kitchen is perfect, especially the plate of eggplant for Sarah. She knows how particular Sarah is about her food arrangement. Once assured that things are running like clockwork in the kitchen, Franc heads out the door and back to the dining room. That's when she notices Kathy speed walking by her on the way to the bathroom, wiping tears from her eyes, and giggling loud enough for the other patrons nearby to hear. Kathy's laughter is so genuine and contagious that Franc can't help but begin to chuckle herself. Wondering what's going on now, she looks toward the ladies' booth. It is clear by the look of embarrassment on Sarah's face that whatever has the ladies in hysterics must have been at her expense.

The sounds of the kitchen are like music to the chefs and cooks. An outside observer might find the scene confusing or intimidating. However, to the people in the dance, it is flawlessly timed, and they are serenaded by the sounds of a living kitchen: the tapping of spoons on plates keeping time, the rattling of glassware adding interest, and the booming of pots brimming with stock moving to and from the stovetop all together creating perfect rhythm. Being familiar with the pace of the kitchen, Sophia takes no pause before making her way around the counter to stand next to Roman at one of the stoves. "You heard him, didn't you? He said she looks perfect," she says with glee.

Moving now from the stove to the counter to plate a sizzling hot steak, Roman is careful not to burn his mother-in-law before he replies, "Yeah, I heard him, but I am not sure what or if there is anything else we can do. You know Franc. She said she doesn't want to get involved with anyone at the restaurant."

"It worked for you and Gina. And now I have four beautiful grandkids to show for it. Besides, what does she know? She's just a kid," answers Sophia with a huff.

"Well, that 'kid' passed forty a long time ago. I think she knows what she wants," says Roman, and then he adds, "She's stubborn, just like her sister." Pausing to look at Sophia, he adds, "Gee, wonder where they learned that."

"Hey, watch it," snaps Mom.

"You're right, sorry. It's just I don't know what you want me to do. We've tried everything. You even locked them in the storage room that one time with the lights off."

"Yeah, I guess that was a little juvenile, but who knew she would get so mad?" confesses Sophia.

"The food critic from the *New York Daily News* was here, and by the time you let her out of the room and she made it to his table, she was sweaty and red-faced from all the time she spent banging on the door."

"She claims it was from banging the door, but we don't have any proof, do we? They might have been smooching for all we know. They've done it before, you know," she says with a wink.

"That was one time over a year ago, and who knows if she's still interested," questions Roman.

"Oh, she's interested. A mom knows these things," replies Sophia with confidence.

Just then Franc walks into the kitchen and finds her mom and Roman in deep conversation and loudly clears her throat to convey her presence. Sophia looks in her daughter's direction, then quickly back to Roman and whispers, "We'll have to come up with a plan another time. Keep thinking, and we'll talk about it later." As she passes Franc, she smiles innocently and says, "Hi, sweetie. We were just going over Christmas gift ideas for Gina and the kids."

Catching her in a lie, Franc can't help but state the obvious, "Mom, it's April."

Sophia simply replies, "Well, one can never be too early to start shopping."

❧

CHAPTER 17

KATHY'S OVERACTIVE BLADDER

Back at the table, the ladies are still chuckling and joking about Sarah's tampon saga as Kathy returns from the bathroom. As the booth shuffle commences one more time, Diane comments to Kathy about how many times she has needed to run to the bathroom. "Why did you sit in the middle of the booth when you know you have to get up to pee every ten minutes?"

Kathy replies simply, "Well, I was here first, and everyone just sort of filled in around me. And besides, I kind of like being in the middle; this way I can bop back and forth from one conversation on one side of the table to the other."

Trying to be understanding, Melissa states, "It's okay, Kathy; my grandma Helen went to the bathroom all the time too."

The look on Kathy's face when she hears this is priceless. There is no need for words; the look she gives Melissa is louder than anything she could ever verbalize. So before anyone can comment, Kathy sends out a warning. "Don't make fun of me today. You have no idea the kind of a day I have had."

"Oh, come on, Kathy. You know we tease because we love you. It's what we do," says Ali.

"I know. And I am thankful to have you in my life, but when I say, 'You have no idea the kind of a day I have had,' I mean you have no idea," repeats Kathy.

Sarah interjects, "Well, it can't be as bad as shoving a piece of cotton candy up your vajayjay."

Kathy tilts her head to the side and utters, "Well..."

⋖⋗

Kathy and Physical Therapy

After the day she had in the ER, Kathy is happy to be heading down to the locker room with her gym bag in hand to get ready for her first day of physical therapy. When Kathy enters the large room lined with red lockers and wooden benches, she is greeted by a middle-aged nurse changing into her scrubs. "Oh, hi, Kathy. Are you on tonight?"

Proudly placing her new pink Nike gym bag down on the bench, Kathy replies, "No, I'm off tonight. I am heading up to the third floor for physical therapy." Then she proceeds to take out the contents of her bag, a pink water bottle, a plum velour tracksuit, and a new pair of white sneakers. Carefully, she places each item neatly on the bench, as if she were dressing a display window in Sports Authority, before opening her locker.

Leaving the room, the nurse says to Kathy, "Well, have a nice evening. I'm on the six-to-six shift. Maybe I'll see you in the morning."

Kathy smiles and says, "Have fun, and good luck out there. It's been a crazy day."

"Thanks for the heads-up," says the fellow nurse before the door has a chance to close behind her.

After changing into her velour running suit, Kathy grabs her water bottle and heads out the door with a little spring in her step to catch the elevator to physical therapy. She hasn't exercised in years, and although she knows Ed loves her just the way she is, she secretly hopes that starting a physical-therapy program will give her just the incentive she has been looking for to finally take off those pesky twenty pounds she's put on over the last few years.

Working such long hours at the hospital, when Kathy gets home, all she wants to do is unwind and spend time with Ed. The last thing on her mind is worrying about a workout routine. This mind-set hasn't just led to weight gain. It has also added a few more grunts and groans when she gets out of bed in the morning as well as added seconds to her response time when running to the ER after a code has been called. Thinking this could be a new start for Ed and her—maybe they'll be like those couples that hike or take yoga classes together on the weekends—she chuckles to herself. "Well, one can only hope."

Kathy arrives at PT and lets the receptionist know she is there for her appointment. As she takes her seat, Kathy looks through the picture window in the waiting-room lobby to see a large room filled with gym equipment and balls just on the other side. She wonders with excitement and trepidation what sort of exercise she'll begin with. "Will it be weights or cardio training?" Smiling to herself, she thinks proudly, "See, you are already beginning to think like an athlete."

Before too long, the nurse comes out to greet Kathy and asks her to follow her to the exam room. Glancing to the right as she passes through the door leading to the patient rooms, Kathy again sees the room filled with the foreign gym equipment and is filled with curiosity. The nurse escorts Kathy down a long hall and into the exam room. There, she takes her vitals and then asks Kathy to step on the scale. Not wanting to see her own weight, Kathy groans and looks away from the scale as she steps on. After writing the vitals in Kathy's chart, the nurse turns to leave and lets Kathy know that Dr. Rogers will be in shortly.

It doesn't take long before the doctor enters the room with Kathy's file in hand. The doctor is a plump, five-foot-two-inches-tall woman in her early fifties, with curly brown hair, glasses, and dimples. She is still reading Kathy's file when she greets her. Looking up from the file for a moment, the doctor says, "I see Dr. Maxwell referred you to us. After looking over your chart, I want to assure you that we will be able to help you with your bladder-control issues."

Relieved by this news, Kathy replies, "That's good, because I don't have time to keep running to the bathroom a zillion times a day."

"Yeah, I know the ER can be a zoo sometimes, especially after midnight. I swear the night brings out something crazy in people." She pauses to add a note to Kathy's chart before continuing. "Not to worry, I am sure we will be able to help you," says the doctor confidently. Then Dr. Rogers hands Kathy a paper gown that she retrieved from the cupboard and instructs Kathy to put it on. "I'll step out into the hall. Go ahead and strip from your waist down, put on the gown, and get on the table. I will be right back."

Kathy, thinking there must be some sort of mix-up, responds in a questioning tone, "What do you mean 'strip down'? I am here for physical therapy."

"Yep," says the doctor as she leaves the room and closes the door behind her without any further explanation.

Reluctantly, Kathy does what she has been instructed to do. Sitting there on the examining table with only the paper gown provided to cover herself, Kathy feels cold and exposed. She wonders what the hell she's gotten herself into.

When the doctor returns to the room, she makes a big show of putting on her gloves: one hand, *snap*, then the other, *snap*. The doctor then plops down on the rolling stool next to the counter, which is across the room from Kathy, and rather than using her hands to move the stool closer to the examining table, Dr. Rogers instead uses both of her feet to propel her chubby body across the room and into the side of the table. The stool makes a large banging sound as it collides with the metal on the side of the table where Kathy is precariously perched. Once there, the doctor gives a sheepish smile and then asks Kathy to lie back. While making continuous small talk, the doctor gingerly puts Kathy's feet in the stirrups, right then left.

Wanting to be any place on earth other than there at this moment and desperate not to make eye contact with the physician, Kathy looks to the ceiling. Staring at the poster of a sandy beach hanging above her, Kathy begins to wonder, "Who ever thought putting a picture on the ceiling for a woman to stare at while her hoo-ha is being prodded was a soothing idea?" She comes to the conclusion instantly; it must have been a man. She can just see it now, a roomful of men sitting around a conference table. "Hey, boys, here's an idea. Let's put a poster on the ceiling of a sandy beach and blue ocean. The women will be so distracted with their daydreaming of a far-off land that they won't notice the cold clamp being shoved up their vaginas. Brilliant!"

"Calming, my ass," Kathy thinks. There is nothing calming about staring at a tropical blue ocean with palm trees while a stranger puts God knows what subfreezing apparatus in your doodad. This quiet tirade runs through her mind as the doctor continues to ask Kathy probing questions. Trying her best to be cooperative, Kathy efficiently answers every question with a one-word answer: yes, no, maybe, sometimes.

After a few moments of small talk, suddenly the doctor stands from her stool and reaches for Kathy. "Okay, let's see what we are working with," states the doctor as she slides a finger into Kathy and asks her to clamp down to see what kind of pressure she's got. Shocked by the doctor's sudden movement, Kathy's eyes widen, and her hoo-ha snaps tight as she almost falls off the table.

CHAPTER 18

SARAH AND LONELINESS

This revelation leaves all the ladies laughing and sputtering, hardly able to control themselves.

"You mean you didn't see it coming? You thought she was done, and then all of a sudden, out of nowhere, the doctor steals third base. She could have at least bought you dinner first," says Ali, laughing.

"Oh my God!" says Diane. "That's what I have to look forward to? We're the same age. This means my time is coming. Ugh!"

"They measure your pressure?" asks Rita, still in disbelief.

"Like a tire gauge?" asks Bette.

"Stop it, you guys. I'm going to have to pee again," says Kathy.

This only makes the ladies roar louder. They tease her and ask all kinds of questions.

"Well, how much pressure is good pressure?" asks Sarah.

Next Melissa asks, "Better yet, what kind of 'homework' do you have? I bet Ed would love to help you with it."

Rita, trying to keep a straight face but failing miserably, adds, "Are you tired from such a hard workout? Did you at least stretch first? We wouldn't want you to pull a muscle or anything else in that region."

Ali can't help but comment on the obvious. "It's not fair. You've had more action today with your therapist than Sarah and I have gotten in the past few months combined."

"Hey," utters Sarah with a hint of indignity in her tone.

Ali replies with a raised eyebrow and a tilt of her head.

"Okay, you're right. It just sounds so depressing when you put it like that," mumbles Sarah.

Kathy begins to join in with the laughter over her absurd appointment, when suddenly a serious look comes across her face. "Oh shit. Now I have to go again. I'm not kidding. Come on, ladies. Scoot." As Kathy leaves the booth and heads toward the bathroom, she can still hear the ladies from across the room laughing about her story.

"Damn it. Now I have to go!" confesses Diane as she hurries out of the booth and heads straight for the ladies' room on the heels of Kathy. This only makes the remaining friends laugh even harder.

During their absence, Sarah begins to let her mind wander to the reality of what Ali said. It really has been a long time since she has been in a relationship. Despite becoming accustomed to doing things on her own, she finds herself increasingly aware of how lonely being single can be, especially during the quiet times, and admits she longs to find someone to share her life with.

<hr />

Sarah and the Movies

Sarah arrives at the movie theater last Monday at precisely 7:20 p.m. for the 7:40 p.m. showing of *The Intern*, a movie by one of Sarah's favorite authors and directors Nancy Meyers. Nancy is someone Sarah considers to be a complete genius; Sarah believes that she has an uncanny grasp on the relationship between men and women and makes it a point to read and see all her works, hoping desperately that through some form of osmosis some of Nancy's wisdom will rub off on her.

The day of the week and timing of Sarah's arrival to the theater are no accident. They are, in fact, a carefully executed plan of attack mapped out by Sarah to avoid notice from the other moviegoers who are on dates. Over the years, Sarah has become good at navigating the waters of being a single woman in New York and at times enjoys the freedom that comes with it. However, she hasn't given up hope or the pursuit of finding Mr. Right.

It has been two years since her last real relationship ended after she and Jeff, another ad executive from her firm, decided to call it quits. There was nothing wrong with Jeff, but there wasn't anything particularly right about him either, and Sarah knew she wanted more. Sarah's whole life has been a series of lists and columns, pros and cons, life goals and timelines. Even as a young girl, Sarah needed things to be in order; she was the type of kid who colored in the lines, kept her desk tidy, and always volunteered to be the teacher's helper. It was these traits that gave her the nickname "Follows-the-Rules Girl" by the other kids in her class. So when the time came to evaluate her romance with Jeff, her decision was an easy one to make.

As Sarah approaches the theater, there are two women ahead of her in line. The ladies all exchange cordial smiles that infer the silent, friendly acknowledgment and solidarity that they, too, are at the movies tonight without a date. A few moments pass, and it is now Sarah's turn to step up to the ticket window, where a freckled-faced girl in her early twenties is standing behind the glass, ready to greet her with the usual questions. "Which movie? Showtime? How many tickets?" But, before the first query can be thrown her way, Sarah is quick to speak. "One ticket for the seven-forty showing of *The Intern*, please. Yes, that's right, I said one ticket. Thank you." After receiving her single ticket from the young girl, Sarah makes her way through the double doors and over to the concession stand, where she collects tonight's dinner; a large bucket of popcorn, a box of Milk Duds, and a Diet Coke. As she makes her way down the hall to theater number five, she sees the lights have been dimmed and can hear the previews have already begun. Happily, she enters in the cover of darkness and makes her way to an aisle seat near the exit.

Giggling as Robert De Niro's character scrambles to get out of the house he and the other interns have just broken into, Sarah turns to the seat next to her, looking to share the joyful moment, only to find it empty. Her smiling face quickly turns somber as she is reminded that there is no one there, no one to hold her hand in the sad moments, nor is there anyone there to share in the laughter.

It is the small things, the everyday things that couples take for granted, that tend to be the largest hurdles for Sarah. These are the times she feels the full strength of the word "*Alone.*"

PART THREE

Dinner Is Served

CHAPTER 19

DISHES AREN'T THE ONLY THINGS HOT AT FRANC'S

Moments later Diane and Kathy return from the bathroom to find Franc accompanied by Paul, one of the waiters, approaching their table. He is carrying a large tray on his right shoulder and a folding table in his left hand. After Kathy and Diane return to their seats, the ladies all watch as Paul, with one smooth motion, places the table down, making it unfold, and then places the tray filled with their dinners on top. He steps back from the table to allow Franc to dispense the food to each of the ladies and heads back to the kitchen to retrieve the next table's order. She places the appropriate plates in front of each of them and again refills their glasses with wine. All is done with the elegance and grace of a well-timed waltz.

"Ladies, I hope you enjoy your dinners tonight. Is there anything else I can get for you at this time?" Franc asks.

Once assured that they don't need anything for the moment, Franc lets Bette and Sarah know she will be right back with their drinks and then turns to leave the booth. But before she can step away from the table, each of the ladies makes a comment of gratitude that assures her how beautiful the meals look and smell. Pleased, she thanks them for their compliments and walks away beaming with pride.

On her way to the bar for the ladies' drinks, Franc passes the bachelorette table and can't help but smile at their behavior. The one wearing the tiara is taking a selfie with her friends but is having difficulty pushing the right button and getting them all in the frame. Clearly this is not their first stop, nor will it be their last on their journey tonight.

While waiting at the bar for Bette's and Sarah's drinks, Franc looks back to take in more of the young girls' show. However, what she sees now isn't so innocent. From her vantage point at the bar, she watches as one of the bachelorette's friends, who's dressed in a slinky tank that leaves no question to anyone looking that she is braless, talks Derek into taking their group's picture. Once done, she asks him to take a seat next to her while they examine the photo, in case they want him to take another. Like any man, he is charmed by their attention, youth, and beauty. So without hesitation, he takes a seat.

Franc's attention is momentarily brought back to the task at hand when the bartender places Bette's and Sarah's drinks on the waiting tray. She thanks him and quickly turns her focus back to the booth. That's when she sees the little ho whisper something in Derek's ear and slide a napkin with her number on it in front of him.

Feeling all the air escape from her lungs, Franc quickly looks away with a million thoughts running through her head. "Are you kidding me? He's old enough to be her father. Gross! And what was that crap he said earlier about me looking 'perfect'? I guess I'm only 'perfect' until a young hottie with perky boobs bats her eyes at him." Realizing how juvenile she is acting, Franc changes her tune. "You know what, forget it. This is totally ridiculous. Why am I getting so angry? I have no control over him. It's not like we're together. Who cares whose number he gets? We only kissed that one time." As her feelings continue to waver back and forth from anger to indifference and back again, she concludes, "I totally made the right decision to keep things professional between us."

Franc turns to look away from the booth before anyone notices her frustration. Unfortunately, she is a little too late. As her eyes meet Derek's, she is faced with the reality of her feelings. It's there in his eyes that she sees the reflection of her jealousy glaring unmistakably back at herself. The expression on his face, however, tells a much different story. It is one that conveys his clear position: "Hey, isn't this what you said you wanted? It's your rule, not mine." Attempting to recover from her stumble, she pulls her eyes from him and leaves to deliver the drinks with her head held high in an attempt to convince him as well as herself that things are better off this way.

CHAPTER 20

BETTE, LAS VEGAS, A MAN, A TATTOO, AND A RING

As the ladies begin to dive into their meals, Sarah discreetly turns her plate so the eggplant is on the left side of the plate and the spaghetti is lined up exactly across the plate on the right side. She then unfolds her napkin, which she lays neatly on her lap, and then straightens and repositions her flatware next to her plate. Starting with the fork to the left of the plate, she moves the handle so it is perfectly straight up and down, and then she moves to the opposite side of the plate, where she adjusts the knife, and lastly, she aligns the spoon.

The ladies of book club are so used to this routine of Sarah's that no one seems to even notice it anymore.

They begin diving into their meals without giving her a second thought. Across the table, without a word to her friends, Bette is also preparing to eat by slowly and quietly taking off her gloves. That's when Melissa looks up from her meal and notices the giant ring on Bette's finger and can't help but squeal in delight, "Oh my goodness!"

Recovering from the ear-piercing scream, Rita looks toward Melissa and asks, "What is wrong with you?"

With her mouth gaping open and unable to speak, Melissa points to Bette's ring. The ladies look to Bette and all notice what has rendered Melissa so speechless. For there on their bachelorette-for-life friend's left hand sits a rock like no other.

Smiling like a Cheshire cat, it's clear that Bette is amused by their looks of surprise and awe. She moves slowly at first, and then suddenly, as though dancing in her chair, she throws her bent wrist forward, exposing the ring in the middle of the table before beginning to tell the story that has redefined her definitions of *love, romance,* and *marriage.*

⇥ ⇤

Bette in Las Vegas

It's been a long and exhausting day for Bette at the writers' convention held at the Bellagio Las Vegas. She decides to stop for a relaxing drink and listen to a little live jazz playing at the Baccarat Bar before heading up to her room. Taking a seat at a small intimate table near the piano player, she orders a glass of crisp pinot grigio. The waiter returns with her drink a few moments later. From her first sip, Bette begins to feel her tiredness of the convention fade away and turn to bliss.

While quietly enjoying her second glass of white wine and the soothing sounds of the jazz coming from the talented and charming piano player, Bette begins to sway to the music. Giving in to the rhythm and alcohol, she lets her eyes connect a little longer than they should with the gifted stranger. When, without warning, she is suddenly jolted back to the reality of the casino when she is rudely interrupted by a group of loud, jocular middle-aged men entering the bar.

It's obvious this is not the environment for this group. "They must have stumbled in accidently on their way from the casino floor, looking for the sports bar," thinks Bette. However, to her surprise and dismay, the men decide to stay. Worse yet, they take seats on the stools at the bar to the right of where Bette was so pleasantly escaping her fatigue of the day. Annoyed by the ignorance of these men talking loudly about their day's adventures gambling and hanging at the poolside when all the while her handsome pianist is trying to elevate his patrons, Bette turns and gives them a look to convey she would like them to keep their voices down. Then, with an overt display of her contempt, she adjusts the chair she is sitting in so her back is now to the men.

One of the intrusive males notices Bette's performance and chuckles at her arrogance. However, to his surprise, he does find her aloofness somewhat alluring. While his friends continue to talk, he continues to be distracted by this stranger. The way she moves to the music is like watching wheat fields swaying in the breeze. Something about her confident attitude, mixed with this grace, renders him mesmerized. No longer able to concentrate on his group of buddies, he gets up and walks to Bette's table. Confidently, he pulls out one of the empty chairs and sits down. He doesn't ask first; he just sits down with his tumbler of bourbon gripped in his left hand. A startled look of shock and disbelief comes across Bette's face, which only makes the intruder's smile even wider.

Bette is taken aback by his rudeness but can't help being a little intrigued by his assertiveness and rugged good looks. He is the complete opposite of most of the men Bette has been attracted to in the past. Deciding to see what this man is about, Bette allows him to stay. With the most saccharine voice she can muster, while adding a sappy, demure gesture for him to sit down and join her, Bette extends an invitation. "By all means, please, take a seat."

He is immediately captivated by her smartass response to his boldness, thinking to himself, "And the dance begins."

What starts out as flirtations and quips quickly gives way to an evening that will define the rest of their lives. They talk for hours, losing all track of time. In fact, neither of them even notices when his friends leave the bar to continue their quest to win back their money and bankrupt the casino. He tells the beautiful stranger that his name is Harry and he is from Manhattan. He goes on to tell her that he is a tugboat operator on the East River. And in return, she introduces herself and explains that she is an author of women's self-help books, coincidently also from Manhattan, and she is in Vegas for a writers' convention.

They continue to see each other for the rest of the week, taking in the sights and sounds of Las Vegas. They do everything from art museums to the lazy river ride at the MGM Grand and main-stage shows to roulette and slot machines without a second thought to his friends or her convention. His gestures of what some might call old-fashioned chivalry come as a pleasant surprise to "the voice of single ladies." Never before has she been with a man who makes her feel so feminine. It doesn't take long for Bette to understand that being a feminist doesn't always mean she has to be in charge, and it is okay to allow a man to treat her like a lady in all its glorious meanings. She understands fully that the way he holds the door for her, allowing her to enter the room before him, and the way he pulls out her chair before sitting at a table and stands when she needs to leave the table are all signs of respect.

On their fourth night together, they find themselves a few blocks off the main strip, standing in the doorway of Old School Tattoos. What starts as a joke during their long visit to Margaritaville suddenly becomes a challenge. Daring Harry to follow her, Bette enters the shop with confidence. Walking up to the guy at the counter, Bette is momentarily distracted by the size of the gauges in his ears but then quickly stays the course and informs him that she and her "friend" are interested in getting matching tattoos. She quickly looks back to see the expression on Harry's face when he realizes she's serious.

With Bette's bold statement, the gauntlet has officially been dropped. Not one to back down from a challenge, Harry informs the attendant that he'll go first. Admiring his style, Bette replies, "Well played."

Moments later, the tattoo artist, a man in his early thirties, introduces himself to Bette and Harry. He says his name is Paul and asks Harry to follow him to his station. Paul is like the poster child for what most people think of when they try to picture a tattoo artist in Las Vegas. He has large metal gauges in his ears where once small round lobes hung, and a skeleton skull tattoo engulfs his bald head, erasing any memory of his once-thick dark hair. The body of artwork ranging from dragons to women wraps his body so that the only trace left of untouched skin is his strong face. Perhaps in another setting, Paul might seem intimidating or unapproachable, but here in his shop, his appearance is a testament to his artistry and craft.

Sitting in the chair, Harry watches Paul prepare his workspace, carefully taking out his sterilized equipment and placing each item on the tray next to them. As the realization of what is about to happen sets in, the urge to get up and run washes over all six feet four inches and 240 pounds of Harry. Just as he is about to make his getaway, he sees Bette's face smiling back at him as if to say, "And the winner is…"

Thirty-five minutes later, Harry's tattoo is complete. The freshly inked pair of dice showing lucky number seven, placed in the inside of his left bicep, is now a permanent reminder of how fortunate he feels at the age of fifty-nine to have found her. What started out as playful banter has grown into something neither one could have ever imagined.

Next it's Bette's turn, and without hesitation, she quickly takes a seat on the artist's tattoo table rather than the chair. As Paul begins to clean his station and prepare the equipment for Bette, he asks where she would like to have her tattoo. She tells him she would like to have the dice placed on her right shoulder blade. She decided on this placement rather than her arm, wrist, or ankle because this is a place on her body only revealed to those she chooses. As Bette loosens her blouse and lies on the table, the tattoo on her left shoulder becomes visible. It is a beautiful depiction of Athena, the Greek goddess of wisdom as well as the patroness of the arts and literature. She is also highly revered for being a brave and fierce warrior, all qualities Bette likens to herself. The tattoo of Athena was just one of the many surprises Bette showed Harry on their second night together. The memory of that night spent together makes Bette begin to blush. When she looks to Harry, the rush of pink streaming across his cheeks tells her without words that he also remembers the same magical night.

Over the next few days, Harry realizes that he has found the love of his life. With their time together in Las Vegas shortly coming to an end, Harry spontaneously asks Bette to marry him, knowing that love like this rarely happens, and if it does, it certainly doesn't give you the benefit of logic or time; it just happens, *wham!*

Somehow, Bette has known from the moment this arrogantly charming man boldly sat at her table her life will never be the same. Confident in her feelings, she surrenders to the knowledge that there is no looking back, only forward together. So without hesitation, Bette hears herself answer unequivocally, "Yes." Bette has always prided herself on being a free-spirited, independent woman who never thought she had any need or desire to settle down. However, over the last few days, she has suddenly come face-to-face with the truth: that she is in love and can't bear the thought of letting him out of her life. Throwing caution to the wind and living in the moment, they are married that night by an Elvis impersonator justice of the peace among all the lights and sounds of Las Vegas.

After five blissful days spent as husband and wife, they returned to their hometown of Manhattan. They had made the decision to sublet Harry's place and have him move into Bette's apartment on the Upper East Side. There they continue to live the quintessential newlywed lifestyle, always a kind word, a soft touch, and a loving gesture, not to mention a very active sex life. They spend the next month enthralled in each other and their new romance, with picnics in Central Park and weekends in the Hamptons.

One morning after a second lingering kiss good-bye, Harry leaves for work, and Bette hurries herself to get ready. She moves about the apartment singing Sinatra and dancing around as if she is in some off-Broadway musical. Her extra enthusiasm this morning is because today is the day she is going to surprise Harry and bring him lunch at the dock. She sashays to her walk-in closet to put on what she considers the perfect nautical outfit in honor of Harry. It is a little something she picked up on her way home from her meeting with her publisher last week. Looking at herself one last time in the full-length mirror propped against the wall in their bedroom, she feels confident about her new outfit. It's a look of the 1950s, navy skirt suit, hat, gloves, and heels. Excited to step into her new role as wife, Bette stops at the local deli and the corner bakery to pick out just the right lunch items, each time proudly announcing to the cashier, attendant, and whomever else she can catch the attention of that she is bringing her husband lunch down at the harbor.

After carefully stocking her picnic basket with the bounty from her shopping spree, Bette arrives at the marina. Making her way down the dock, with their lunches in hand, she scans the docked boats for Harry. Spotting him just a few slips away from the main walkway, with a huge grin on her face, she waves and yells with glee to Harry and his crew, "Hello, boys!" Bette smiles a little extra as she recognizes one of Harry's crew members from the Vegas group. Hearing Bette's voice, Harry proudly jumps from the boat and onto the dock to meet his wife. When he reaches her, he takes her in his arms and passionately kisses her, reminiscent of Bergman and Bogart from *Casablanca*. Then he answers with a strong, sultry, "Hello, Wife."

CHAPTER 21

ONE LOVE STORY BLOSSOMS WHILE ANOTHER ONE CRUMBLES

B ette tells the ladies step-by-step how they met in Las Vegas and how Harry had the audacity to sit at her table without asking for her permission first.

"I can't believe it. He just sat down?" asks Melissa.

Sarah adds, "I would love it if I could find a guy that would take charge like that. I mean approaching your table and sitting down without being asked, so confident and manly." She makes a guttural tiger sound. "Rawrrrr. Now, I could really go for a guy like that."

"Sounds like a good piece of pork." Kathy chuckles.

"Oink, oink," says Bette, laughing, and then gives a wink. Bette tells them how she was first intrigued by his rugged good looks and self-confidence and later fell in love with his kindness, humor, and passion. Next she tells her friends about the adventures they went on while away and how she played hooky from her conference and he skipped out on his friends. Strengthening the story of her fairy-tale romance, Bette boasts about their nonstop sex life, which the ladies can't get enough of, and brags that she is more satisfied now at sixty-one than she ever was in her twenties.

Melissa comments, "I hope Ryan and I are as frisky as you two are when we are your ages."

Surprising her friends with another confession, Bette confesses, "Oh, and we also got matching tattoos."

"Shut up!" screams Ali.

"You didn't?" questions Rita.

Bette nods yes while boldly replying, "We did!"

Ali is the first to ask, "What did you get? And where did you put it?"

"Okay, don't laugh. We got matching tattoos of a pair of dice with a five and a two. Harry says it is for lucky number seven. I know it sounds corny, but it represents how lucky we feel to have found one another. He put his on the inside of his left arm, and I put mine on the back of my right shoulder," explains Bette to the captivated table.

"Awe, I don't think it's corny at all. I think it's sweet," fawned Diane.

"You totally have to show us. Take off your shirt," says Melissa with wild eyes.

"Are you crazy? I am not taking off my shirt in the middle of Franc's," replies Bette.

Kathy, taking charge of the situation, insists, "Oh yes, you are." Then she orders the group, "Ladies, make a wall."

As if instructed by their military leader, the friends, in perfect formation, construct a fortress of bodies and napkins, granting Bette the freedom to lower her top enough to reveal her tattoo to the group.

While adjusting her top, Bette notices a woman two banquettes over glaring at her in disapproval. Bette doesn't hesitate to shout to her, "Oh, get over it. This is New York. Like this is the worst thing you've ever seen." Now muttering just loud enough for her own table to hear, she adds, "You frigid prude."

"Bette!" Melissa scolds like a mother.

"Eh, don't worry about it. A little dose of reality is good for her. She'll get over it," defends Bette.

Looking back now to Bette's tattoo, Sarah says in admiration, "That's so cool. Way to go, sister."

Diane comments, "Harry got the same one? That's so romantic."

"Truth be told, I think he thought I was bluffing when I told him I thought we should get them," confesses Bette.

"What did the guy doing your tattoo think when he saw the two of you walking into his place smelling like tequila and asking for matching tattoos like a couple kids on a twenty-one run?" asks Rita.

Sarah quips, "Yeah, I bet he looks at his parents in a whole new way now."

"He probably thought we were a little nuts, but who cares what he thinks? It's Vegas, baby. Why should the kids have all the fun? Besides, we're like two old bottles of wine; we only get more interesting and better with age," says Bette proudly.

Kathy boasts, "Oh, age has nothing to do with it. Ed and I have been married for ages, and we still manage to keep things interesting."

Rita beckons, "Go on."

Kathy explains, "Well, a few months ago, I completely shocked him when we were in bed together."

Sarah, intrigued, asks, "What did you do?"

"Let's just say there is no more hair from here down," replies Kathy as she points to her head, grinning from ear to ear.

"By gone, you mean everything's gone?" inquires Sarah.

Kathy proudly answers, "Everything!"

"Everything?" questions Sarah again, just to be clear on what she has heard.

"Yes, my friend. Everything. I'm talking Telly Savalas everything," confesses Kathy.

Melissa, now getting in on the questioning, exclaims, "No, you didn't! What did Ed say?"

"He said he wanted to keep the lights on!" Kathy blushes.

Rita says with a smile and a raised glass, "I am impressed. Ed is a lucky man, my friend."

Diane interjects, "Forget Ed. Tell us, what do *you* think about your new do?"

Kathy indulges her friend's request. "To be honest, I think it's kind of fun. I mean it kinda makes me feel sexy. Especially the first few days, there is nothing there to cushion your lady parts, so you feel everything. I mean everything. But for sure the best part about the change down south was surprising Ed. I like keeping him on his toes. He never knows what to expect from me. Now don't get me wrong. I'm not saying I'm going to keep it this way forever, but for now, it is fun." With a change of her tone, she admits, "However, the upkeep is ridiculous. I mean by noon I have a five-o'clock shadow. If only my hair on my head grew as fast as my areas south of the equator, I would have hair down to my butt by dinnertime each night."

Bette quickly adds, "Well, not only do you have to keep up the maintenance for Ed, but now don't forget about your newfound lover, your PT doc. I'm sure Dr. Rogers likes a nice clean canvas to work on."

"I know, right? Who wants stories of their stubble going around the hospital's break room?" says Kathy with real concern in her voice.

After an unsolicited litany of grooming techniques from the group and between bites of her lobster fettuccini, Bette reveals to her friends that there is one thing about getting married that has her feeling a little anxious. And that is, what will her agent and her readers think when they find out this self-proclaimed eternal bachelorette met the love of her life in Las Vegas and eloped?

"Oh, don't be silly. You have nothing to worry about," Sarah assures her friend. "They're going to be happy for you." She then raises her glass and makes a toast in Bette's honor. "So here's to new beginnings and new voices."

Melissa seconds Sarah's opinion and adds, "Your fans are loyal. They love you for your strength, honesty, and wisdom. That doesn't change just because you're married now."

"Yeah, now you can show them a new side of you. And I know they're going to embrace this new journey of yours with open arms and lots of book sales," says Diane in support.

"Cheers," the friends say in unison as they take a drink to tribute Bette.

Amid the goodwill, Ali notices that Rita is suddenly being very quiet and asks, "What is it, Rita? Is everything okay?"

Rita, trying to smile but with tears swelling in her eyes, confides in the sisterhood of her friends a statement that takes everyone by surprise. "I think Jim is having an affair."

Taken aback by this announcement, no one speaks for what feels to Rita like an eternity. They sit there in silence, completely unsure of what to say next or how to comfort their friend. It's Kathy who finally breaks the silence. "Oh, sweetie, what makes you think Jim is cheating on you?"

Trying to hold back the flood of tears, Rita looks down at her glass of wine, not wanting to make eye contact with anyone. She knows that if she sees the hurt and concern for her reflected in her friends' eyes, she will surely fall apart. She has always prided herself on her strength but knows at this moment she is close to crumbling. She fears that if she lets even one tear fall, she might never stop. Holding on to her wineglass as if it were her lifeline and running her hand up and down the smooth stem, she takes a deep breath and begins telling them what has really been going on in her life...

━━━◈◈━━━

Rita's Marriage

In the kitchen of their newly renovated three-bedroom condo in Tribeca, Rita is getting breakfast ready and making the morning coffee. Rita's husband, Jim, walks into the kitchen and goes over to the cupboard near to where Rita is standing and pulls out a coffee mug for himself and then closes the cupboard door without saying a word. They are so used to their morning routine that it's almost like a silent dance of sorts. She steps one way and he the other, staying out of each other's way, careful to never touch.

As they sit together at the granite breakfast bar in the kitchen, they take out their phones and begin their morning ritual of going over the day's appointments and schedules. Rita clearly points out each of their appointments and gives her unsolicited opinion on how long each should take. Her belittling demeanor makes Jim feel like a junior employee rather than a partner and co-owner of their real-estate brokerage company.

They have two twin sons, John and Michael, who are seniors in high school. The boys both have busy schedules of their own, filled with school, homework, and varsity soccer. Family is very important to both Rita and Jim, and they strive to make their sons a priority every day. However, when it comes to their own relationship, they have lost all sense of what it means to be a couple. At this point, they are basically roommates who have kids in common.

When the boys enter the kitchen to grab a quick bowl of cereal, Rita focuses on them. She goes over each boy's schedule for that day in detail. "John, you have a US history quiz in second period, and, Michael, don't forget to ask your Spanish teacher about making up the vocabulary quiz you missed last week because you were home sick. Dad and I will see you at the soccer game tonight. Oh, that reminds me. Don't forget to bring your uniforms with you today, because the bus leaves directly from school for the game," rattles off Rita, barely taking a pause to breathe.

Feeling the constant tension between their parents, John and Michael gulp down their cereal as quickly as they can, drop their bowls in the sink, grab their backpacks from the backs of the kitchen stools, and head for the door. Looking back at their mom and adding a courtesy smile, they say in unison, "Yeah, yeah. Got it. We'll see you guys at the field. Bye." They both hurry out the door before any more can be said to them.

With the boys gone, Rita's attention is now brought back to Jim, who is still sitting on the stool at the bar, looking over his appointments for the day along with some paperwork from his briefcase. She is quick to remind Jim of the start time of their boys' soccer game. Frustrated with Rita's tone and demeanor, he answers sharply, "Of course, I know what time the game is. I haven't missed one yet, have I?"

Ignoring Jim's response, Rita unnecessarily reminds him that he needs to get going because he has a closing this morning at the title company across town. Jim, feeling hurt and frustrated with her patronizing attitude, doesn't give her a response. Instead, he methodically gets up from his seat and puts his plate and coffee mug in the sink. Then he walks over, picks up his papers, places them neatly back in his briefcase, and leaves for work in his passive-aggressive way of warfare.

Rita is all too familiar with Jim's retreats but is too numb to react. Exhausted from the constant fighting, she longs for the days when things were easy between them. She feels hurt watching him gather his things to make his abrupt, silent exit, but what can she say this time that she hasn't said a hundred times before? At this point she doesn't know anymore if it's her pride or insecurity that stops her from confronting him, surrendering to the reality that sometimes it's just easier to let him walk away.

Jim makes his way to the elevator and pushes the down button. The elevator doors open, but Jim is unable to move. He waits and watches as the doors close in front of him. Tracing his memories, he tries to remember when things began to change between his wife and him. When did things go so wrong? One day they were a happily married couple in love, and now it seems the only time she talks to him is when she is patronizing or criticizing him about one thing or another. He's noticed that tensions in their home have gotten so bad that the boys seem to leave every chance they can get in order to not be caught in the cross fire.

Convinced that something has to change, he walks back into the condo with hopes of connecting with Rita or at least telling her how he has been feeling. Maybe then they can start to mend whatever it is that has broken their marriage and friendship. He makes his way through the living room and into the kitchen, but unfortunately, when he gets there, he can see Rita is already fast at work on her phone with a client. She doesn't even look up when he says her name. "Looks like she didn't care, or maybe she didn't even notice that I left. Why am I not surprised?" These are just a few of the thoughts running through his mind. Feeling alone, Jim retreats and walks out the door once again.

When the door to the apartment closes behind him, the truth is revealed in the tears running down Rita's face. There was no client on the other end of her phone. She just didn't have the energy or the strength to fight, and she knew if he saw she was speaking with a client, he wouldn't push the issue.

Later that day, Jim arrives early to his sons' soccer game and parks in the gravel lot nearest to the field. He finds great pride in watching them and always tries to get there early enough to watch the teams warm up. Looking onto the field from his car, he admires his boys for the strong athletes they have become. "Wow, they have come so far." He can remember watching them run up and down the field in their peewee soccer league just like it was yesterday. It was so amusing watching the herd of little kids cluster around the ball, not knowing how to dribble let alone shoot for the goal.

As he walks to the field, he can see other husbands and wives already standing on the sidelines, waiting to see their own sons battle the opposing team. As he approaches, the parents greet Jim with smiles and small talk before focusing their attention back to one another. While standing there, Jim looks around and notices a clear contrast to his own marriage because these couples all still look like couples. He watches as they talk to one another, catching up on the day's events. They stand next to each other, affectionately joking and giving an occasional flirtatious touch or teasing hip bump. They share things like umbrellas and get each other coffee, and believe it or not, they actually smile when the other one is talking, like they are truly interested in what he or she is saying. This observation only makes him feel worse about his own relationship, knowing how things used to be. He questions again to himself, "How did we get to where we are? I remember being madly in love with Rita. We spent every moment we could with each other. There was a time when she used to smile when I looked at her. Now we are no more than coworkers and roommates, and at times not even friendly coworkers." Feeling defeated, he turns his attention back to the field and the game that is about to start.

Rita arrives a few minutes after the game has begun. Parking her car in the vacant spot at the far end of the lot, she runs to the field. She feels so disappointed and angry with herself for not getting to the game earlier. This will be another time she has to explain to both the boys and Jim that she couldn't help running late. She was showing an apartment and couldn't get away. "At least I made the sale. Maybe this time they will be happy about that," she hopes.

When she reaches the field, she sees Jim on the opposite sideline, near midfield. Instead of going to stand with him, Rita is so caught up in the game and watching her boys play that she continues to stand on the sideline where she came in. It isn't until halftime that she makes her way around the field and over to Jim. As she gets there, instead of greeting him with a hello, she immediately begins defending why she was late. She explains to him that she just couldn't get away but for a good reason; she put the Sanders' place under contract. Then, before Jim has time to respond, she asks him if he remembered to open escrow for the Jacobs' condo.

To Rita's dismay, there was no congratulations on the sale, but instead what she got was his usual retreat. "I need to return a phone call," he says and then quickly walks downfield without looking back.

When the game resumes, Jim joins Rita and the other parents on the sideline. Remembering he is there for his sons, he makes a good show of cheering and supporting the team, but Rita can tell he is upset and fears it is her fault yet again. Throughout the second half of the game, Jim never utters a word to her. Like so many times before, she continues to push him away. Thoughts of self-doubt and confusion flood her mind. "Why do I do and say the things I do? Why can't I just relax? I don't need to always be in charge. Jim is a good man. He is competent, smart, kind, and most of all, he's a great dad."

Stealing glimpses of him without letting him notice as he cheers for John and Michael, Rita is reminded of how much she loves her husband and wishes things could be easier between them. She knows she needs to do something before it is too late to save her marriage. She can't remember the last time the two of them spent an evening together without it ending with one of them angry or upset. So as the game draws to an end, Rita musters up her courage and abruptly turns toward Jim and asks if he would like to get dinner together tonight, just them, alone, without the boys. Surprised by her invitation, Jim hesitates before answering, "Sure." Hoping the feelings of nostalgia will ease the tension between them, Rita suggests they go for Chinese at the Hong Kong Garden. It's the restaurant Jim took her to twenty-one years ago on their first date, a point that is not lost on Jim when he hears her suggestion.

The ride to dinner is spent in cordial conversations, mainly recapping the highlights of the boys' game. They arrive at the restaurant with high hopes for the night, but unfortunately it doesn't take long for both of them to be disappointed. Somewhere between the egg-drop soup and almond chicken, they each quietly come to the same conclusion that they have lost all ability to just be together as a couple and enjoy one another's company. They find that once they run out of small talk—work and the boys—there really isn't anything left to say. So the remainder of the dinner and the car ride home are spent in an awkward silence. Both Rita and Jim know the deafening silence is saying more to them about their marriage than either of them is ready to admit.

CHAPTER 22

FRACTURED MARRIAGE AND A WHITE WEDDING

Melissa says to Rita, "I don't understand. Jim and you have been together forever. You always seem so happy together. I see you all the time around the school, and Jim plays racquetball with Ryan every other week. He's never said anything to Ryan. I'm so sorry. Really, I had no idea."

"You couldn't have known. I never wanted to admit it to anyone. Somehow I thought that by not actually saying the words out loud, I could still pretend that everything is okay…that my marriage is okay…that I am okay," says Rita with quiet reflection. Looking down to her wineglass again, Rita continues. "I know we look fine when we are out, but when we are alone, we have nothing to talk about. Maybe it's because we work together all day. I mean we are together at home, then all day at work, and then back at home together again. Each day is the same. Maybe he is bored or just sick of seeing me all the time. I don't know." Admitting more than she thought she would to herself or her friends, she adds, "Or maybe I am the one who's bored with him. I don't know what came first, but I do know we have lost the talent to connect with one another as a married couple should."

"No, that can't be it. Sweetie, you are wonderful. He should feel lucky to spend so much of his day with you," replies Sarah.

"All I know is that Jim doesn't smile at me like he used to. We used to love spending our days talking for hours about real estate, dreaming of opening our own brokerage and starting a family. Well, we did it all, and now look at us. I can't even remember the last time we had sex," confesses Rita. "I swear I think it's been about six months. And you know what the really upsetting thing is? He's not complaining. I remember when we were first married, if two days went by, he'd give me the look, like 'Hey, it's been a while,' then kiss my neck as he passed me in the kitchen, and I knew that it meant we were going to *you know* later that night. And now, nothing, not a look, not even a touch as we pass each other in the hall or kitchen. I mean nothing. No holding hands in the car or sitting by each other on the sofa late at night when we're watching a movie. I mean absolutely nothing. I'm afraid he's getting his needs met some-where else," she adds.

"Six months?" Kathy asks in disbelief.

Rita tries to justify it. "Our lives just got so busy. Between the boys and the brokerage, we are so tired that by the time we finally make it to bed, either I am too tired or he is too tired. So we just kept putting it off, until we got to the point where we even stopped talking about it," admits Rita.

Trying to be an optimist, Diane replies, "Well, you said it yourself. You guys are exhausted. I'm sure that's why he's not approaching you."

"I'd like to think that's the reason, but last week he said he was going to drive by a potential listing on his way home. Sounds fine, right? Well, that 'drive-by' took two hours, and I swear I could smell the faint scent of alcohol on his breath as he passed by me on his way to the bathroom," answers Rita.

Ali says half jokingly, "I know a PI. We did a piece on him a few years back. I can have my assistant look up the number for you. Then we can find out for sure if Jim's getting his, as you put it, needs met on the side." Grabbing her handbag to dig through to find her phone, she adds, "If you'd like, I can give my assistant a call right now and have her look it up first thing in the morning. Do you want me to call her?"

Rita smiles and says, "Thanks, but I don't think I am ready to take it to that level yet, but I will keep you posted."

Then she excuses herself to use the bathroom and get a few moments of privacy to try to collect herself.

Stunned from the bombshell Rita has just dropped on them, they aren't sure how to react. Allowing Rita her space, the friends sit in silence as she walks away.

A few minutes later, Rita returns from the bathroom, composed and ready to rejoin her friends. Despite her brave face, it is clear to her friends that she has been crying. While soft words of kindness and support are given to her from everyone around the table, a beautiful couple walks up and interrupts. It is an attractive gay couple in their early forties, each fit and sporting just the right amount of gray peppered throughout their perfectly groomed hair. One of the men is dressed in a pink oxford top and khakis and the other in a cable-knit sweater with tailored pants and Prada loafers. Perhaps better than their look is the way they smell. It is a combination of the ocean and flowers, clean, beautiful, and intoxicating. Diane introduces her gentlemen clients to her friends as the men thank her for the gorgeous floral arrangements she did for their wedding last month at a beach on Montauk.

Watching the couple walk away from the table, the ladies turn their attention now toward Diane. They wait in anticipation, knowing she will have some story to tell them. As predicted, as soon as the men are out of earshot, Diane gives the ladies what they are waiting for, the scoop on the couple's wedding.

"It was truly the most beautiful wedding I have ever seen!" Diane gushes. "Every aspect of the wedding was done to perfection. Cliff, the taller one, is a true stickler for detail. He had his say in everything from the flowers to what the guests were wearing. In fact, he was so involved in the planning of their big day that he, the wedding planner, and myself met on so many occasions to discuss the flowers that we naturally became friends. So much so that Cliff extended an invitation for me to attend the wedding, and I, of course, didn't hesitate to say yes!"

"Seriously, you have the best life," concedes Melissa.

Sarah inquires, "What did you have to wear? No matter what it was, it has to be better than the stupid bird Beth had strapped on the side of my head."

Diane replies happily, "Everyone wore white. Per their request, everything was white, and I mean everything. Not only the guests but the flowers, the candles, the chairs, and the tents were all white. Even the walls of the event tent were draped in white silk with enormous crystal chandeliers covered with pearls hanging throughout the room. Cliff said I wasn't allowed to use greenery in the floral arrangements either. So I had to spray all the foliage white—stems, leaves, all of it, white.

"I'm telling you—it was absolutely stunning. The only color in the entire place was worn by the grooms. They had on matching gray suits with a single pink rose in their lapels. Even their beloved dogs that stood up front with them for the ceremony were white," adds Diane in awe. "The whole event had a soft glow from the candles. Oh, and the multiple strings of small white lights covering the tent's ceiling created this elegant sparkle that danced across the tent as they reflected off the hundreds of crystals hanging from each chandelier. With the fresh scent of the flowers in the air and the roar of the ocean in the background, it was perfection. Even the dinner they served was white. I am telling you everything on my plate was white: fish with white-wine sauce served with a side of white asparagus and rice pilaf. The cake was a seven-tier white-chocolate-and-buttercream work of art. Believe me, I have done hundreds of weddings, but I have never seen anything like this. Seriously, it was absolutely exquisite. There is simply no other word to describe it."

CHAPTER 23

SOPHIA AND THE RESERVATION

The phone at the podium in the busy waiting area rings three times before Sophia has a chance to answer it. "Ciao, *Franc's*, Sophia speaking. How may I help you this evening?"

"Hi, I'd like to make a dinner reservation for five," replies the woman on the other end of the line.

Looking through the reservation book, Sophia replies, "Um, let me check to see what we have available." She pauses to scan the page. "Looks like the earliest opening we have is in a few weeks, on Thursday, May 27. We can seat your party at eight. Will that work for you?"

"Perfect," says the woman with relief.

After taking down the caller's name and phone number, Sophia asks if they are coming in to celebrate a special occasion. Confused and intrigued by the caller's answer, she can't help but continue to ask more questions. "You're celebrating a fifty-year challenge? Well, that's the first time I've had anyone say that to me. What is it?"

"My girlfriends and I are all turning fifty this year. Well, three of the five of us are. The other two already paved the way for us. Anyway, we made a pact to use this year to challenge ourselves to do something we've always wanted to do," explains the caller.

"Oh, that sounds like fun," Sophia says gleefully.

The woman quickly rebuts with sarcasm. "That's what I thought too, until I heard about all the crazy things my friends had in mind. You see the caveat surrounding this brilliant idea was that all five of us had to do each of the challenges together."

With trepidation, she agrees, "Oh, that is an interesting twist."

Hearing the sympathy in the hostess's voice, the woman responds with gratitude, "I know, right? You wouldn't believe some of the things these ladies and I have done this year. But I am happy to say we all lived through it, some of us more battered and bruised than the rest, but nevertheless, we lived through it and are ready to sit and celebrate our accomplishments."

Eager to hear all about their adventures, Sophia closes by saying, "Thank you for choosing *Franc's.* I look forward to meeting you and your friends. We'll make sure you have a special evening."

CHAPTER 24

ALI AND MR. WONDERFUL

As a young waiter comes and clears the book club's table, Ali lets out a loud burp, which makes Rita, Melissa, and Bette start to giggle. Kathy reacts to the bodily function as if she were talking to her own child. "Ali?"

"What?" Ali says with a smile and then laughs. "Really, my friends, you don't know what my life has been like these past few weeks and all the stress I have been under. You've all heard me gripe about my *wonderful* producer, Stanley, a million times over the years. Well, Mr. Wonderful continues to be the fly in my pudding. He's made it his mission to not let me forget my contract is up for renewal. Ladies, I am seriously worried. There are so many young, hot twenty-somethings biting at my heels, just waiting for an opportunity to take my job. I've been trying to play it safe for a while now and not make too many waves, but I don't know how much more I can take. You wouldn't believe some of the humiliating crap Stanley has me doing on air recently in order to stay, as he refers to it, *fresh* and interesting to the younger demographic, in hopes of raising the show's ratings."

Bette, sympathizing with her friend's situation, can't agree quickly enough. "I have to admit, I've seen a few of your pieces lately. I'll just say they're not the most riveting."

"Oh, I don't know. The one you did last week on how long it takes before beer loses its fizz when left on the counter was pretty important information," Diane says with a chuckle.

"Diane!" Melissa scolds.

"What, I was trying to lighten the mood," answers Diane innocently.

Ali doesn't miss a beat or even make eye contact. "Yeah, so you know what I'm talking about!" she says as she continues her rant on ageism and the fleeting attention span of pop culture.

Allowing her the space to vent, each of the friends waits for Ali to pauses to catch her breath before giving her words of encouragement. They also remind her that she is just as beautiful as the day she first started on *Good Morning New York*, but more importantly, she is smart and respected throughout her professional field of journalist colleagues. Being sure to make the point that doing a few fluff pieces won't change that.

Although Ali loves and appreciates their show of support, these last few months she hasn't felt as if she is smart, respected, or relevant in the television-news world anymore. She carries on telling them about the absurd pieces she has been doing for the show, all in the name of "good TV."

"Did you guys see the piece they had me do on what celebrities name their babies? I mean, really, who cares if Kim and Kanye named their baby North West or Gwyneth has a daughter named Apple? What do I care? I think time could be better spent on reporting things that are a little more important, don't you? Like I don't know, how about the mass genocide in Rwanda or the great Pacific garbage patch or maybe—"

Ali stops midstream in dissertation about the downfall of our modern-day society. The expression on her face changes suddenly from anger to bliss as she sees Franc approaching the table and knows she is there to take the group's dessert order. Ali has been fantasizing about what she is going to order all week and can barely contain her joy.

Melissa informs Franc that they've all decided to share a couple of desserts: a slice of cheesecake and tiramisu. Apparently all, that is, except for Ali, because before Franc has a chance to walk away from the table, she adds to the dessert order. "Oh, and I will take a slice of the chocolate decadence cake. Thanks, Franc." Knowing better, the ladies keep quiet about Ali's additional order.

As Franc leaves the table with their orders in hand, Bette revisits the conversation with Ali. "I can't believe that moron has you doing those kinds of brainless stories. You've been to the White House to cover the past two elections for Pete's sake, and now they want you to talk about the latest way to fight wrinkles. And who really cares who the new teen heartthrob is this week? I mean really. They need to get their priorities straight."

"Seriously, you've done some important work," adds Kathy. "A woman with your experiences should be respected and revered, not tossed aside for a newer, younger version."

Melissa seconds that thought, saying, "Exactly! You are precisely the type of person I want to get my news from."

Ali responds with self-doubt, "Yeah, but we aren't in an election year. And Stanley says no one wants to hear too much about what's really happening in the world first thing in the morning while they are drinking their coffee and trying to rush out the door for work. He's afraid it depresses the audience, and then he fears they will change the channel to find more lighthearted news stories." Ali continues her self-deprecating attitude by pointing to her less-than-perky chest. "Preferably one hosted by a cute young thing with boobs that still point upward." She adds, "Someone who reports on things like the red-carpet hits and misses and who wore it best or how to find the perfect pair of jeans that will lift that sagging butt of yours or how to plan the perfect wedding on a budget."

"That's bullshit. You're an award-winning journalist, and your age should be seen as an asset, not an obstacle. It shows you have experience," says Diane with conviction.

Rita interjects, "Have you thought about moving to another station or program that would appreciate the great news reporter you are rather than this morning show pandering to the sensationalism and Hollywood celebrity youth running amuck? I mean really, Ali, you sound more upset about the misplaced news content rather than the sexist ageism running rampant in Hollywood." Shaking her head in anger, she adds, "Wow, hard to say which of those injustices pisses me off more."

Ali answers emphatically, "I am fed up with both!"

"I bet there would be producers ringing your agent night and day if they knew you had an interest in leaving *Good Morning New York*," states Melissa with certainty.

Sarah chimes in, "I agree with Melissa. Maybe you should put out some feelers and see what happens?"

Pausing to listen and absorb what her friends are telling her, Ali says with conviction, "You know what? You guys are right. What the hell am I doing? I shouldn't have to lower myself just because Stanley can't keep up with me. Screw him and *Good Morning New York*. I do deserve so much more. Thank you. I needed to hear this. I'm going to call my agent first thing in the morning and tell her to start putting the word out that I want out."

"Now that's the Ali we know and love," says Rita.

"You go, sister," toasts Diane while raising her drink to Ali's.

Kathy smirks. "I wish I could be a fly on the wall to see Stanley's face when you tell him you are leaving… priceless!"

"Knowing what a weenie he is, I bet he cries," says Bette, chuckling.

PART FOUR

Desserts, Drinks, and Goodnight

CHAPTER 25

BATTLE OF THE WITS

While gathering the ladies' desserts from the kitchen, Franc runs into Derek, who is on his way to the floor. "I see your little friend had to go," she says sarcastically. "Aw, is it her bedtime already? It is a school night after all."

"Ha-ha, very funny. She's actually older than you think," answers Derek.

"Oh, I bet she is." She nods with a smirk. "I'm sure you two will have a lot of things to talk about. Just make sure to have her back before her curfew."

Derek gives a sly smile with his response. "Well, don't worry about it. Besides, what I do or do it with really isn't any of your business now, is it?" As he begins to walk away, he pauses and whispers in her ear before leaving the kitchen, "Remember, you're the one who wants us to be friends and nothing more."

Unable to return a well-suited quip in his direction, Franc slams the tray of desserts down onto the counter in a huff, frustrated over the thought of him leaving and feeling as if he has gained the upper hand in their never-ending battle of wits. In an attempt to gather her composure, Franc closes her eyes and begins to count to ten. When that doesn't work, she closes her eyes even tighter and continues counting.

CHAPTER 26

DRINKS, DESSERTS, HEARTBREAK, AND BONDING

Moments later, Franc returns to the table with fresh cocktails for Bette and Sarah and, most importantly, the desserts for the table. While she is there, Franc also takes the opportunity to refill the empty wineglasses before walking away. The friends' attention is distracted from the importance of morning TV and is now focused on the plates of goodness that have just been delivered: raspberry cheesecake and a wedge of tiramisu, not to mention the sizable slice of chocolate heaven, which has Ali practically drooling.

With her mouth still full of Brenda's chocolate delight and frosting on the corners of her mouth, Ali moans and says, "Oh my God, I have died and gone to heaven."

Melissa takes the first bite of the cheesecake. She closes her eyes. "Yum." But unfortunately, Melissa's excitement of raspberries and sweet cream cheese is cut short. To her horror, she looks down and sees a big red spot on her new gold sweater, and panic instantly comes across her face.

"Oh, don't worry, honey. I am sure it can be cleaned," says Sarah.

"Sure it can," adds Kathy. "You can't believe some of the stuff I have gotten on me, and the cleaners always get it looking good as new."

With her eyes brimming with tears, Melissa explains to her friends that she's not upset about the sweater; it's because Rachael had asked if she could wear it when she goes to the movies next week with a couple of her friends. "You don't understand, she's never asked to borrow anything of mine before." She lets them know how hard it has been lately for her, trying to navigate the rough waters of parenthood and friendship, and how she feels she and Rachael are entering that transitional period where they are going from mother and daughter to more girlfriends and confidantes. She tells them about what happened the other night when she and Ryan came home from the PTA meeting to find their daughter crying. She goes on to tell them how Rachael's boyfriend had just broken her heart and how hard it was for Melissa to see her baby crying. She also tells them how the night ended with Rachael and her staying up all night talking and that somewhere between their tears, they found laughter together. She admits that this was the first time Melissa realized her child had grown into a young woman with hopes and dreams of her own and was no longer her little girl. Happily, she adds that this was also the first time Melissa let Rachael see the woman she is, not as a mom but as a woman and a friend with her *own* independent hopes and dreams for the future.

Melissa's Life

On the way home from the PTA meeting at her daughter's high school, Melissa can't stop smiling. "That went really well, don't you think?" she asks Ryan.

"It was great. Everyone liked your idea of having the seniors' graduation party at the boathouse on the harbor." Then Ryan adds, "See, I told you there was nothing to be nervous about."

Happily, Melissa agrees, saying, "I know you were right, but I couldn't help it. I thought for sure Leena Ericson was going to fight me on the location. I know she thinks it would be better at the Le Grand, but really, a hotel on senior night...what was she thinking? She might as well be handing out condoms and room keys to each of the kids along with their diplomas. Besides, I think the chaperones will have a much easier time watching the kids at the boathouse. There really aren't too many places the kids can sneak away to."

A short drive later, they arrive home. Melissa is still wearing a smile on her face for a job well done when suddenly her feeling of euphoria quickly turns to concern as they open the door to the apartment and hear crying coming from their daughter's bedroom. Melissa turns to Ryan with a confused look on her face and whispers, "What?"

Ryan shrugs his shoulders and mouths the words, "I don't know."

"Rachael, honey, what's wrong?" questions Melissa as she makes her way down the hall to Rachael's room.

Without a word, Rachael runs from her room to her mom's open arms. There in the hallway, Melissa stands holding her daughter, comforting her. A few moments pass before Rachael stops crying long enough to explain that her boyfriend, Justin, broke up with her. She goes on to tell her mom that Justin said he likes the new girl, Sheila Anderson, and that he is going to ask her to go with him to the senior prom.

Ryan attempts to make Rachael feel better by kissing her on top of the head and stating, "It's okay, honey. We never really liked Justin anyway. Don't worry. You have a couple of weeks before prom. I'm sure you can find another date."

In unison, Melissa and Rachael pull away from their embrace to look at Ryan with an expression that conveys that they think he is a complete idiot. Melissa can't believe what he just said and is having a hard time not letting out the rage that is running through her mind. "Is he stupid? You don't tell your daughter that you never liked her boyfriend. For all we know, they could be back together next week, and then what do we say? And don't worry about the prom? Good grief!" She continues her silent chastising, thinking, "Doesn't he know how important prom is to a girl or how long it took them to find the perfect gown and shoes? You don't just find another date two weeks before prom, you moron. Who will be left at this point? Prom dates have been set for months. Seriously, how can he not know these things?"

Taking his unspoken cue from the ladies, Ryan decides to retreat to the family room to watch some sports before making any more blunders. He concedes to the fact that he is clearly no help in this situation, knowing there are just some times in a girl's life when she needs her mom.

Armed with the appropriate breakup foods of potato chips and ice cream with homemade fudge sauce, Rachael takes a seat on a clear acrylic barstool at the kitchen's marble peninsula. While Melissa is at the stove making each of them a fat mug of Mexican hot cocoa with just a hint of cayenne pepper, Rachael begins telling her mom the whole story. Rachael starts by telling her how Justin texted her during fifth period and said he needed to talk with her after his baseball practice this evening and how after school Genni called her to ask how she was doing after the breakup. Rachael was totally caught by surprise with Genni's call. "I didn't know what Genni was talking about. I had no idea that Justin wanted to break up with me." Rachael continues to explain how embarrassed she felt. She is convinced Justin must have been going around school telling all his friends he wanted to break up, and she had no idea. She feels like a fool and wonders how many of the other kids knew of his plan before she did.

"Of all the girls, Sheila Anderson, why her?" asks Rachael in frustration. "What's so special about her?"

"You know that British accent she flaunts around so proudly probably isn't even real. I bet she isn't even from London. She's probably from someplace normal, like Nebraska," snarks Melissa.

Thankfully, Melissa's sarcasm makes Rachael laugh and helps to change the tone for the rest of the evening. Both mother and daughter stay up all night talking about boys and life. To their surprise, somewhere in the course of the night, their tears turn into laughter and smiles. At one point, Rachael optimistically says she knows a guy in her calculus class who doesn't have a date, and she thinks maybe she will see if he wants to go with her.

The rest of the night they bond over stories of Melissa. The teenage years, stories of her loves won and lost, not to mention the many fashion disasters on her quest to fit in at school. It's fun for Rachael to think of Melissa as a young girl and not just her mom. As the night wears on, their talk develops into something more meaningful and real than either of them could have imagined hours earlier when the evening began.

Rachael states with a newfound awareness, "Okay, enough about Juuuuustiiiiin. Seriously, if that coward doesn't have enough respect for me to tell me that he wants to take someone else to prom before spreading it around school, then good riddance. Sheila can have him. I'm better off without him."

Melissa responds proudly to her daughter's stance, saying, "Absolutely, if a guy doesn't treat you with respect, then he's not worth your tears. Besides, you'll have a much better time going to prom with a friend rather than a boyfriend anyway. Trust me, I know what I'm talking about."

Wanting to know more about her mom, Rachael asks, "You never really talk about your childhood or Grandma Carol, how come?"

"Well, as you know, when I was growing up, Carol was not the same person that you got to know. The Carol that I had was a completely different one from the person that sent you birthday cards or remembered to send you gifts at Christmas. The Carol that I grew up with was an alcoholic and an abusive wreck."

"Sorry, I didn't mean to make you sad," says Rachael.

"No, it's okay. I am happy that my mom finally got the help she needed and that we were able to have some sort of relationship before she died. I just wish she would have gotten sober earlier. We lost so much time that could have been spent together," says Melissa, remembering her childhood.

Being a stay-at-home mom may not be the right fit for some, but for Melissa, it means everything. Having grown up in such an unstable environment herself, Melissa wants nothing more than to give her daughter the childhood she always longed for. "I know there have been times in your childhood where I may have seemed a bit overprotective or been a little too smothering, but I want you to know I had the best intentions," admits Melissa to her daughter.

Poking fun at her mom, Rachael replies, "Okay, sometimes I do think you can take things a little too far. Like, remember the time you showed up at my seventh-grade gymnastics meet wearing a sweatshirt bedazzled with 'Rachael's Mom' on the back and carrying pom-poms?" Raising her left eyebrow for more emphasis, she continues, "Carrying pom-poms. Really, Mom, what were you thinking? Now, that was a bit much, but I always knew you did dorky stuff like that out of love."

"Gee, thanks. When you say it like that, I should win a Mother-of-the-Year award for sure," says Melissa with sarcasm and humor.

Rachael responds in a more serious tone, "Okay, but really, how many kids do you know who still have their moms make them cookies on the first day of school, even when they are in high school, or how many of them know the names of all their friends? All joking aside, I really do think you're a great mom." Smiling softly, she adds, "You know I'll be heading off to college in the fall. I think it's time for you to do something for yourself."

Pausing to reflect on what her daughter has said, Melissa admits, "Well, there is something that I've always wanted to do."

Intrigued, Rachael asks, "Really?"

"Now, don't laugh, but I've had a dream to one day open up my own French bistro," divulges Melissa.

"Laugh, why would I laugh? I think it's a great idea. What's stopping you? Do it!" exclaims Rachael without a moment's hesitation.

"I don't know. It would take a lot of my time away from you and Dad and the house," acknowledges Melissa.

"Look, Mom, Dad and I are fine. It's time for you to take care of yourself. Do something that you love to do. I see the way you look when you're in the kitchen and how happy it makes you to see people enjoy your creations. You were meant to do this. I think you should go for it."

"I don't know," says Melissa nervously.

Building her mom's confidence, Rachael adds, "I think it would be totally cool. You'd be so good at it. And think about it; you can bring home all the leftover desserts...you know Dad would love that!"

"Maybe you're right. Your dad and I have been talking about me opening up a small place of my own off and on for years, but the timing never felt right. Like you said, you're going to be heading off to college in the fall, and I'll have all this free time on my hands. This might be the perfect time," says Melissa with a sparkle in her eye at the thought of actually doing it. "Wait here. I will be right back. There is something I want to show you." Then Melissa disappears down the hall to her bedroom.

From under her bed, Melissa pulls out a dusty black box covered in white peonies. The box is filled with her mementos from throughout the years, old love letters from Ryan, an old student ID from college, and other various items that hold great sentiment from her earlier years with Ryan. Among the items in the box is a worn envelope that Melissa takes out and cradles in her arms before placing the lid back on the box and returning it to its slumber under her bed.

Back in the kitchen, Rachael is sipping her hot cocoa when Melissa returns and, with a smile on her face, hands her the envelope.

"What's this?" asks Rachael.

With enthusiasm in her voice, Melissa replies, "Just open it."

Doing as she is instructed, Rachael opens the envelope and pulls out the content. It is a napkin from Melissa's favorite French restaurant. On the napkin is a sketch of a small restaurant with the name "La Nourriture" written across the front of the awning in scrolled black letters. Before Rachael can ask a question, Melissa begins telling her the story of the evening Ryan and she spent at a small bistro, drinking wine and dreaming of the life they would build together as husband and wife. Ryan had been offered an internship for a job in Manhattan with Mathew and Olson Architects right after graduating from college.

Melissa knew how great this opportunity was for Ryan to live among and study the buildings he had admired as a student from afar. For it had just been a year earlier that

Melissa herself had dropped out of school in her junior year at Western Washington University to pursue her own passion of becoming a chef. When Ryan was offered the internship in Manhattan, Melissa was attending culinary school in Seattle. They both agreed to take on this new adventure together. Melissa applied and was accepted to the International Culinary Center in SoHo, and within just a few short weeks, they got married, packed all their belongings, and headed east in a used Suburban packed to the brim. Their honeymoon was spent camping and sight-seeing along the way.

Once in New York, they found a small studio to rent and lived a very modest lifestyle on their shoestring budget. On their first anniversary after arriving in the city, they had saved up enough money to go out for a decadent meal to celebrate. Over a bottle of cabernet sauvignon and plates of rich food, Ryan spoke of his desire to one day be a renowned architect known for combining old-world craftsmanship with modern-day design. Melissa, in turn, told Ryan of her dream to someday open her own small bistro much like the one they were dining in. It would be a place where she would create an atmosphere that made each customer feel as if he or she had been transported to the French countryside, a place where she would make all the customers who came to partake in her cooking feel as if they were sitting around the family table at their grandma's house for a Sunday dinner.

It was then that Ryan took a pen from his pocket and drew on Melissa's napkin. He drew a quaint restaurant, complete with flower boxes filled with fresh herbs and flowers and an inviting striped awning to beckon patrons in. He handed Melissa the napkin and promised to one day make her dream of opening her own bistro a reality. It is the most beautiful and precious thing Ryan has ever given her. She named her restaurant La Nourriture.

CHAPTER 27

MELISSA EMBRACES A NEW CHAPTER IN HER LIFE

Melissa's story is met with praise and admiration. Talking to her all at once, the ladies tell her how thrilled they are that she is finally seeing herself as the woman they have always known she is, someone who is confident, smart, and creative.

"Wow, I can't believe you saved the napkin all these years. That is so romantic," gushes Diane. "I can't wait to tell Chad. He is going to eat this up."

Rita, not one to skip a beat, adds, "I can totally help you find a place. We can start the search first thing tomorrow."

"Whoa, I think I need a little time to do research before I can commit to a location, but thank you. What do you say we start shopping for a spot in a couple of weeks?" asks Melissa.

"It's a date. We can go for drinks after," answers Rita.

With a smile on her face, Diane asks to join them on the search. "Drinks and shopping sound like fun. Sign me up."

Bette chimes in, "What do you think about coming over next week and teaching me how to make beef bourguignon for Harry? It is our one-month anniversary next Friday, and I would love to surprise him with a meal like his mom used to make for him."

Melissa adds, "Oh, Bette, I would be honored. I have a great recipe. I make it all the time for Ryan and Rachael; they love it. It's really easy too."

"Thanks. I'm new at this whole cooking thing and I can really use all the help I can get," admits Bette with all honesty.

"Don't worry, I've got your back," replies Melissa to Bette, adding a wink.

Turning now to address all her friends, Melissa says, "You know I have to admit it feels a little scary, but good to be embarking on a new adventure. Don't get me wrong. I have loved every moment of parenting, and I wouldn't change a thing, but Rachael doesn't need me like she used to. That part of my life is over, and I'm starting to realize that it is okay for me to be looking forward to this new chapter."

Kathy interjects, "I think it is wonderful for Rachael to see her mom doing something so truly courageous. She must be so proud of you for following your dream."

Ali says with admiration, "We all know you're a good mom, but I think I speak for everyone when I say that it's about time you started putting yourself first for a change."

Encircled by her friends' love and support, Melissa realizes how different her life is now from the one of her childhood. She smiles, knowing how blessed she truly is.

Melissa's Childhood

Melissa grew up on what was referred to as the lettered streets of Bellingham, Washington. In the mid-1970s, it was one of only a handful of housing areas a single mom could afford. She lived in a modest turn-of-the-century Victorian in the 2100 block of C Street from the time she was four until she left for college at eighteen. Her mom, Carol, had a good job at one of the local banks, where she was able to work her way up through the years from teller to vice president of the home-loan department. To the outside world, Carol looked great, but behind closed doors she was a very different person.

From the first time she can remember, Melissa has always had to fend for herself. By the time she was in the first grade, she was putting herself to bed at night and getting herself ready for school on her own most days. She also learned at a young age to know what was waiting for her each day after school by the positioning of the drapes in the front window. If they were open, a sigh of relief would wash over Melissa because she knew this meant her mom was still at work. But if they were closed, it meant Carol would be waiting for her when she opened the door, sometimes with venom and other days not. It depended on how much vodka her mother had consumed that afternoon.

Her mother wasn't always a mean drunk; her mood correlated with how empty the bottle or bottles were. When she was just partway through her first bottle, Carol felt free. This was when she was the most fun. On these days, she would take Melissa on adventures, sometimes to the beach to find clams and starfish, other times to the park to collect leaves and flowers. Her mom loved music, the louder the better. On many occasions when Carol was feeling loose, she would take Melissa by the hand and declare a dance party in the middle of their kitchen. They danced and laughed for hours. These are some of Melissa's happiest childhood memories.

Winter was Carol's favorite time of the year; she loved the snow. One time when Melissa was just seven years old, she woke at three in the morning to her mom, joyfully intoxicated, pulling at her and telling her to get up and come outside. She slurred, "The snow is the perfect condition for making snowmen. Hurry up, sleepyhead. Get out of bed. The snow won't wait forever." They had a great time that early morning in their pj's, boots, and coats. Melissa remembers the laughter coming from her mom as she tried to lift the heavy round head atop their enormous snowman and how cold the snow felt in her small, bare hands.

However, on the days Melissa came home from school to find the curtains drawn closed, it usually meant she would be met with the dark side of vodka. It was on these days Melissa tried hard to enter the home without being discovered, quietly opening the door and making her way to her bedroom, careful not to wake the monster who was passed out on the sofa.

Other times Melissa was met at the door by her mom, half-dressed with a tumbler of liquid hatred swaying in her right hand. Carol never let the demon all the way out, stopping herself just short of physical abuse. In spite of being invisible to the outside world, these verbal lashes cut deeply and left a lifetime of scars on Melissa's young body. Melissa remembers her mom blaming her for her father's absence. At times she claimed that pregnancy had ruined her body, and that was why Melissa's dad had left. Other times she said he left because Melissa was an ugly, hateful baby, adding that it was her constant crying that drove him away.

On these nights when Carol was at her worst, Melissa took refuge in the bathroom until her mom either passed out or finally left her alone because it was the only room in the house with a lock. Some nights Melissa would also run the water in the tub to help drown out her mom's litany of screaming profanities and the repetitive booming sounds of her fists against the door.

Like most alcoholics, the next day Carol was always full of remorse, begging and pleading for Melissa to forgive her, bargaining and making promises. Melissa knew her mom would never keep any of them. Most of the time, this included Carol making a big show of throwing away bottles of booze and promising that this time she was going to stop drinking for good. On these days her mom also cleaned the house and cooked real dinners, not their usual diet of fast food or pizza.

The dinners were the real treat, because they didn't happen very often. In fact, there were many times Melissa would go to bed hungry. Thankfully, during the academic year, Melissa was guaranteed two meals a day, breakfast and lunch, provided by the school. These were oftentimes the only meals she would see. The weekends were sometimes hard, especially on the occasions when Carol would go on a bender and leave on Friday and not return until Monday. During these times, Melissa would either go hungry or learn to use what she had available to make a meal. She quickly discovered that she could make tomato soup from catsup and hot water from the tap. It wasn't very tasty, but it was warm, and it filled her belly, if only for a small time. Melissa also learned to save part of her meals from school. She hid them in a box in her dresser for the times when the cupboards were bare.

When Melissa was in the sixth grade, a couple and their two-year-old daughter moved in next door. They were the first lesbian couple Melissa had ever seen. By all accounts, they were a typical traditional couple. Mary went to work each day, and Lori stayed home to raise their daughter, Grace. Walking home from middle school each day, Melissa looked forward to seeing Lori playing with Grace in the front yard, observing how patient and kind she was with her young daughter. As Melissa passed their yard, she would bend down to say hello to Grace and pat her on her golden curls. Lori would ask about Melissa's day at school: what she studied that day, if she had a lot of homework, how her friends were doing. Melissa remembers how good it felt to have someone care enough to ask about her day and listen to her stories of her classmates and friends.

As the school year went on, Melissa's daily stops at the neighbors' yard grew longer and longer. Some days Melissa would sit on their front porch, telling Lori all about her day while watching Grace play in the grass. The world next door was so different from her own that Melissa wished she would never have to leave.

On one of their visits, Lori surprised Melissa when she asked if she would be interested in a job. She offered to pay Melissa to come over after school each day to help with Grace, explaining that she needed to repaint the front porch and could use some help keeping an eye on their active toddler. Melissa knew Lori didn't really need her help, but despite the pretense, she was happy to go along with the charade. It didn't matter to her whether it was the yelling at all hours of the night, or the unkempt yard, or the heaping mountains of empty vodka bottles that overflowed the garbage can each week that made it clear to Lori that she needed to be saved. The only thing that mattered was that there was someone in the world who truly cared about her well-being, and she was grateful for the compassion. Melissa's time spent at the neighbors' quickly grew from one to three hours a day, allowing Melissa to stay for dinner. Another added bonus with this new job was the money. With the income she made helping out next door, Melissa was now able to have fun riding her bike downtown to shop at the market or pay for a bus ride to Lake Whatcom to meet her friends.

At the end of her freshman year in high school, Melissa applied for a job at Dairy Queen. It was just a little under a mile from her home, an easy distance to walk or ride her bike. The application needed her mom's signature in order to allow someone under sixteen to work there. Melissa had been forging her mom's signature for so many years that this was no obstacle, and within no time she found herself behind the counter selling soft serves and burgers. Over this summer, Melissa had changed. Not only did her new job grant her the ability to buy trendy clothes, makeup, and music like the other girls were buying, but her body changed as well. So much so that when school started up again in the fall, Melissa was no longer the tall, awkwardly skinny girl hiding in the back of the classroom, trying desperately not to be noticed. Instead, she was now a beautiful, fully developed young woman who couldn't help but stand out in a crowd. The next three years of high school, Melissa's popularity and confidence continued to grow. She was nominated homecoming princess of her sophomore class and made varsity cheer her junior and senior year.

In complete contrast to her high-school life, things at home continued to decline. Carol was spending more days drunk than she did sober, and her attendance at the bank was random at best. While the other girls at school were going on shopping sprees for senior prom dresses with their moms, Melissa was busy cleaning up her mom's messes and trying to keep her safe.

When graduation finally arrived, it was no surprise that Carol was nowhere to be found. However, to Melissa's delight, sitting prominently in the auditorium were her neighbors Lori and Mary with their daughter, Grace, cheering her on. Seeing them there meant the world to Melissa, for over the years, they had become her substitute moms, confidantes, and friends. Later that evening, after the ceremony came to an end, Melissa arrived home to find it once again lonely, dark, and empty. Even though she knew better, she had still held out hope that Carol would be there, ready to congratulate her on her accomplishment. Unlike so many of her classmates, she had no graduation announcements sent to relatives, no graduation party, no graduation gift, and no celebration.

It was later that week that Melissa moved out from her mother's house and into an apartment with a friend from work. She was now old enough to be on her own, independent, no longer tied to her mom and all that encompassed her downwardly spiraling lifestyle. Confident and strong, Melissa left the house on C Street and never looked back or shed a tear. It would be another ten years before Melissa accepted any contact with her mother, and that was only after considerable persuasion from

Ryan because he thought it would be good for Melissa to let her mom know she was going to be a grandmother.

Melissa continued to stay close to her old neighbors Lori and Mary over the years through letters, Christmas cards, and phone calls. They watched over Carol and gave updates to Melissa about how she was doing. It was during one of these phone calls that Lori informed her that Carol had enrolled in a court-mandated AA program after passing out behind the wheel on her way home from the bank. This incident was the catalyst for what would become a healing process between Melissa and Carol.

After two years of sobriety, Carol reached out to Melissa. And over the next twelve years, she made great strides in repairing some of the damage she had done throughout Melissa's childhood. On two occasions Melissa flew Carol out to New York to introduce her to Ryan and Rachael. Melissa is so proud of the life she was able to create for herself in spite of her upbringing. She wanted to show her mom what her life is like and introduce her to her friends. But most importantly, she wanted to let her mom know that she is okay and no longer holds any grudges.

Six years later, Melissa would find herself sitting on a flight, heading to Bellingham, Washington, flanked by Diane and Rita. The three women are on their way to pick up Carol's ashes and settle her estate. Melissa had received the call from Lori six days earlier, informing her that her mom had died in a car accident. Ironically, the accident was the result of a drunk driver running a red light and hitting Carol on the driver's side. Hearing the tragic news, Ryan reached out to Melissa's closest friends. His first call was to Rita. She, in turn, notified the others in the group. Without waiting to be asked by Melissa, both Rita and Diane made arrangements with Ryan to accompany her to Bellingham. In that moment, sitting between her friends and knowing her husband and daughter were seated in the row behind her, Melissa began to understand the true meaning of support, friendship, and family. Family doesn't always mean the people you are related to; sometimes it means the ones you hold closest in your heart. "Thank you for coming with me," she says with tears in her eyes.

Diane, looking to Rita, replies, "We wouldn't have it any other way."

CHAPTER 28

SARAH AND CHARLIE

Among the well-wishes for Melissa's new adventure into the culinary world, Sarah can't help but be distracted when she looks up from her martini to see an amazingly handsome man walking by their table with someone who appears to be his wife. Noticing the attention from Sarah and the number of wine bottles on the table, the handsome stranger innocently smiles and nods to the ladies with admiration as he walks on by as if to say, "Well done, ladies."

"Now that is a good-looking piece of pork," drools Ali as he walks by.

"Why can't I find a man like that? I swear all the good ones are taken. Did you see his smile? That's what I am looking for," says Sarah with a twinge of jealousy.

"Speaking of which, how are things going out there? Any luck with the online dating?" asks Diane.

"Well, I did go on a date last week," confesses Sarah.

Bette blurts out, "Come on. Spill the beans. We want the whole story. How was it? Where did you go? Are you going to see him again?"

"Did he get further than Kathy's physical therapist?" says Ali, chuckling.

Happy for her friend, Rita adds, "Yeah, tell us everything."

"Especially the *R*-rated parts." Kathy laughs.

Sarah begins, "Let's just say online dating is now a four-letter word in my book."

"With a statement like that, now you have to tell us," says Melissa, pushing the subject.

Giving in to their prodding, Sarah finally relents. "Okay, but I'm telling you it wasn't exactly a fairy tale." And with that, Sarah starts her online-dating dissertation as her friends settle in to hear a story they know they will thoroughly enjoy.

Sarah's Dating Life

It's eight o'clock in the evening when Sarah finally arrives home after a long day at the office. Happy to now be at home, stripping out of her heels and constricting business attire, she changes into something a lot more comfortable. From the long dresser that sits under the window in her bedroom, she pulls out her favorite pair of pajamas, the ones with the tan-and-light-blue-striped bottoms and matching blue camisole. She then makes her way to her closet and finds her favorite oversize, comfy, cable-knit beige cardigan. Sarah smiles with luxurious contentment as she slips her arms through the armholes, feeling the soft cashmere knit against her body. The oversize sweater is more like a cozy blanket rather than clothing wrapping around her small frame.

In the bathroom, she washes off the day's makeup and stress before heading out to the kitchen to pour herself a much-needed glass of merlot. Soon after she puts the cork back in the bottle, the doorbell rings. To her delight, it is the Chinese takeout she ordered on her way home from the office.

When Sarah opens the door, the delivery boy greets her by name and once again asks her the same question he asks each time: "Hey, Sarah, how's it going tonight? Got any big plans for the weekend?" She is mortified to admit that she has, yet again, no plans for the weekend. There's no date, no party, just herself, a bottle of wine, and reruns of *Grey's Anatomy* on Netflix. She doesn't dare let him in on her spinster lifestyle. Instead, she lies and says she has to work.

Sarah orders Chinese takeout from the Golden Dragon so often even the hostess who answers the phone recognizes her voice. "Oh, hello, Sarah. Combo number four, again?" On one hand, Sarah feels it is a little embarrassing, and on the other, she likes the familiarity. It's quaint that in a city as large as Manhattan they can be so intimate with one another. Fortified with her food and wine, Sarah is ready to settle into her Wednesday-night routine. She positions herself on her midcentury olive sofa, with the glass of red wine in her left hand and an open laptop perched on her lap. Between sips and bites, she scrolls through her online-dating account, looking at each potential candidate. Disappointed as usual by what she sees, Sarah begins making snide remarks about each guy's profile to humor herself.

"Right, 'career change.' What you really mean to say, Jeff, is that you are out of work."

Going to the next candidate/victim and then another and another, she shoots each one down before moving on. "Let's see what we have here. Marc, he's okay looking." Scrolling through his accomplishments, Sarah sees he actually wrote, "Drives a Lamborghini." "You know what that means—small penis. No thanks, Marc—moving on."

Finally, she sees one post that interests her. "Well, hello there, Warren," she says with a smile. After reading through his profile a few times just to make sure there isn't something she's missing, she finally concedes to the astonishing fact that she can't find anything concerning or alarming. Happily, she sends him a message and then waits nervously for a reply. To her surprise, she gets a response back almost immediately. Through a few data-gathering inquiries sent back and forth, she finds out that they have a lot in common. They actually grew up not too far from one another, and when they were younger, they both had a family cat named Fluffy. After a few days of what seems to be very promising messaging back and forth, Sarah decides to accept his offer to meet for dinner, and they set the date for the following weekend.

Saturday finally arrives. Her first date with Warren is just hours away, which has Sarah both excited and utterly nervous. Everything up until now, the messaging and talking on the phone, has been easy, but tonight is different; they will be meeting in person. She hopes they will have something to say to each other and that he's not one of those guys who only knows how to communicate through the safe distance of typing or calling and can't actually hold a conversation face to face.

Preparation for the big date is an all-day ritual for Sarah, starting with exfoliating and shaving her legs and then moving on to trimming and grooming her special lady parts. Once out of the shower, a complete full-body coat of moisturizer is a must. Then she is on to polishing her nails, both hands and feet. While allowing time for her polish to dry, Sarah moves on to perhaps the most important preparation of all, picking out the right outfit, one that says she's not too easy but not too uptight either. However, it also has to be something that conveys that if things are going well, she just might *be* that easy. After much deliberation over dress pants with a revealing blouse or a skirt with a silk tank bejeweled with a hint of glitz in the neckline, she settles on something in the middle, a formfitting, low-cut, little black dress with gold jewelry.

Now to find the right undergarments; hidden under her usual sea of beige is what she is hunting for, a sexy black pair of panties with matching bra accented with pink satin and lace trim. They are what she optimistically calls her good-luck charms, and she is hoping they won't let her down tonight. Sarah catches a glimpse of her reflection in the mirror above the dresser while grabbing her unmentionables. "Well, you never know. Tonight might be the night," she says out loud to the woman staring back at her as if she were cheering on a friend.

Sarah and her blind date agreed to meet at The Loft restaurant because it is halfway between both their places, and more importantly, it comes highly recommended by Melissa. As she puts it, the food is over the moon, and the chef is renowned for using only local, sustainable items for their menu. True to her character, Sarah arrives to the restaurant fifteen minutes early.

The hostess lets her know she is the first of her party to arrive and then leads Sarah to their reserved table near the window.

Seated alone at the table, Sarah anxiously begins looking around the restaurant while fidgeting nervously with the table settings, waiting for her date to arrive. When Warren does arrive on time, Sarah is not disappointed in what she sees. Amazingly, he's as good-looking in person as he is in his profile picture. Over a shared bowl of clams as their starter, Sarah begins to relax and finds she is really enjoying herself. To her delight, the date is going well; he is handsome, funny, and charming. She can't help but begin to wonder why such a great guy is still single, a question that will unequivocally be answered a few mere moments later.

While the waiter clears the empty bowl once holding the juicy clams and their small appetizer plates, Warren asks Sarah if she minds if he checks in quickly with the sitter. He explains that he is usually home to put Charlie to bed and just wants to make sure everything is going well. Sarah knows from his profile that he is a single dad and replies, "Oh, of course, go ahead." Giving him privacy, she adds, "I'm going to step into the ladies' room. I'll be right back."

When she returns from the ladies' room, Sarah is a bit surprised to find Warren is still on the phone with the sitter. After taking her seat, Sarah whispers with concern, "Is everything okay?"

He covers the receiver on his phone and explains that the sitter is having trouble getting Charlie to sleep. He then asks the sitter to put Charlie on the phone. Once his son is on the phone, Warren proceeds to sing Charlie a lullaby, right there in the middle of the restaurant. Sarah is so embarrassed by the impromptu concert being held at her table that she doesn't quite know how to react. She continues to sit quietly, thinking, "This surely can't go on all night." Thank goodness after fifteen minutes and nine verses, the lullaby seems to have worked; Charlie is finally asleep. Satisfied with a job well done, Warren hangs up the phone and looks across the table at Sarah. He then asks if she'd like to see a picture of Charlie.

By now Sarah is sick of hearing about Charlie; however, not wanting to appear rude, she replies, "Sure, I'd love to." Warren proudly opens his wallet to show her a picture of his beloved Charlie. Only then does Sarah realize that Charlie isn't a child at all but, in fact, a ferret. A long furry rodent with beady eyes! Mentally, she answers her earlier question, "Well, now I know why he's still single." Immediately, Sarah hands Warren back his wallet. Placing her napkin on the table, she quietly stands up, slides her chair under the table, picks up her handbag from the back of her chair, and, with all the composure she can muster, says to Warren with certainty, "I think we are done here." Without hesitation or another word, Sarah walks away from the table, Warren, and the restaurant to hail a cab.

CHAPTER 29

DATING AND WHOLE FOODS

"Are you kidding me?" asks Melissa, trying hard not to burst out in laughter.

Sarah replies, shaking her head, "I can't make this crap up!"

Diane can't contain her laughter any longer and shouts, "The beloved Charlie is a ferret!"

Wanting to be sensitive to their friend but overcome by the sheer absurdity of the situation, the ladies erupt in laughter.

"Seriously? A ferret? He sang a lullaby in the middle of a restaurant to a rodent?" chimes in Rita.

Kathy exclaims as she pushes Rita, Ali, and Bette out of the booth and knocks down two books on her way, "I can't take it. A ferret. I am going to pee my pants. Let me out!" At this point, the books knocked to the floor are just casualties of war, obstacles cluttering her path to the bathroom. On her way to the restroom, the ladies can still hear Kathy laughing and shouting, "A frickin' ferret!" from across the room.

"It's not funny!" protests Sarah.

Rita replies, "Oh, sorry, sweetie, I have to say, it really is."

"My friends, you have no idea what it is like out there," demands Sarah. Then she goes on to explain her experience in the world of online dating. She complains about the fact that so far all the men she has met online are not at all what their profiles say they are. However, it hasn't all been for naught, because after all the failed attempts at finding her perfect mate, she has become quite fluent in the art of men's deceptive profile descriptions. "For instance," she says while looking around the room, "take that guy over there, the ancient man with the younger woman. His profile would read, 'I like to keep my relationships private,' a.k.a. married."

Looking around the room, she spots her next victim. It's a young couple sitting at an intimate table for two close to the bar. It is obvious by the nervous look on the young man's face that this is their first date. "He clearly dressed up for this date," she says, pointing out his stiff new jacket and bow tie. "I bet his profile says, 'Lives with two roommates,' a.k.a. his parents." Next Sarah points out a man in his early fifties sitting at another table, on a date with a young, beautiful girl who looks to be in her early twenties. She observes how the arrogant jerk is openly flirting with the waitress while touching the leg of his date under the table. "His profile reads, 'Looking for someone with an open mind,' a.k.a. someone interested in three-ways and freaky sex."

Impressed by Sarah's knowledge, Melissa curiously asks, "Do me next. What would my profile say?"

But before Sarah has a chance to give Melissa her reading, Ali interrupts, inquiring, "Dry spell, huh?"

"Dry spell is nothing; it's like the desert. You have no idea how long it's been since I've been on a decent date, let alone had sex," complains Sarah.

Trying to arouse a smile, Bette blurts out, "You mean, with something that doesn't require a battery."

"Well, what can I say? I would rather go to bed with my rabbit than a guy with a ferret infatuation," concedes Sarah.

Diane is quick to add her two bits to the conversation, saying, "I agree my rabbit is the perfect date. He never complains about my grooming or wants to stay for breakfast the next morning."

"I've taken to trolling Whole Foods for a little male attention," confesses Rita.

Surprised by her statement, Kathy questions, "You do what?"

"Whole Foods. It's an untapped market," answers Rita.

Skeptically Diane responds, "I thought meeting men in a grocery store was just an urban legend."

Blushing, Rita admits, "I did too until I experienced the wonderment for myself. It feels so good to be flirted with. In fact, I've been there so many times in the past two weeks that I swear I half expect the manager to announce over the store's intercom, *'Attention, customers, we have a special running today on a middle-aged woman in aisle nine desperately looking for some male attention.'* Now, just so we're clear, I'm not saying I would ever act on it, but it does feel *so* good to know that someone still finds me attractive."

Ali, eager for help, pleads, "Yeah, yeah. We know you love your husband and wouldn't do anything to jeopardize your marriage, but what we really want to know are the details. Store location? Time of day? You have to give us your secret." Looking toward Sarah, she says, "Sarah, take notes. We can use this kind of info."

"Good idea, we'll team up. The more players on the field, the better the odds," agrees Sarah.

Looking her friend up and down, Ali says with a straight face, "Yeah, I don't think so. I'm not competing with that body. I say we divide and conquer. You can have Mondays and Wednesdays and I'll take Tuesdays and Thursdays. What do you say, deal?"

Happy to hear someone has noticed how hard she's been working at the gym lately, Sarah replies with a smile and a handshake, "My friend, you have a deal."

Turning her attention back to Rita, Ali orders, "Okay, now enlighten us."

Rita and Whole Foods

Parking her car next to the cart return, Rita grabs her handbag from the passenger seat and heads for the doors of Whole Foods. Once inside she makes her way to the salad bar to grab a little dinner before going home. It's been a long, hard day at the brokerage firm with the sale of the Bennett home falling through due to a failing inspection. Knowing she is the only one home for dinner tonight because the boys are at an away game and her husband is showing properties, Rita thinks a run through the salad bar and a quick stop down the wine aisle is just what she needs to turn her day around.

Standing in front of the mixed greens, she is suddenly aware of the body emanating the strong scent of cologne standing close to her. As she moves down the row to gather fresh peas, she feels him move to keep her same pace. When she rounds the end of the bar, she senses him still on her heels. Annoyed by this invasion of her space, she can no longer keep quiet. "You're welcome to go around me."

"No, it's fine. I'm in no hurry. Ladies first. Take all the time you need," he says with a smile.

Irritated with his response, Rita has no choice but to put the tongs down and walk away before she says what's really on her mind: "This isn't the school cafeteria; you don't need to stay in line. Idiot."

Stopping by the dairy section on her way to her blessed wine, Rita pauses to pick up a gallon of milk before going over to the coffee creamer section. Reaching in to grab her husband's favorite flavor, her hand is suddenly blocked by another. Startled by his touch, she immediately reacts by saying, "Oh, sorry."

"That's okay," the stranger says with a smile.

Then, as if the first time wasn't bad enough, they again both reach for the same creamer. Fed up with her day at work and the morons who apparently shop at six o'clock on Mondays, Rita walks away making a mental note to never go to Whole Foods at this hour again. She rounds the corner of the wine aisle, and her mood begins to lift as she rationalizes, "Okay, so I only have half a salad for dinner tonight. Not a big deal, I'm saving a few calories. And I don't really care that Jim is out of his creamer. I'm sure he can rough it for one or two days making do with plain old milk and sugar."

Waiting in line at the express lane, the man in front of Rita turns toward her to make small talk. Looking at her wine selection, he comments, "Have you had that before. I've been told it's really good. I'm going to have some friends over this weekend. I just live around the corner. Maybe I should give it a try?"

Not really paying much attention to what he is saying, Rita replies, "That's nice," before checking her phone for missed calls.

The line at the register moves, and it is now time for Rita to check out. Emptying her basket onto the conveyor belt, she hears the cashier begin to ring her items and then ask, "Not your type, huh?"

Unclear if she heard the young man clearly, she responds, "Excuse me?"

He continues his question without pause, "You know. The guy, not your type?"

Puzzled by his query, she asks, "What are you talking about?"

The clerk gives Rita a look to convey the expression *"Are you kidding me?"* before stating the obvious, "You didn't notice? Come on, he practically asked you to marry him. You think he slipped in the fact that he lives around the corner and is having a party this weekend on accident? Don't worry, I'm sure you'll find what you're looking for next time."

Confused, she tried to make sense of what he said. "Next time? What was this kid talking about?" As she begins to look around the store, she notices the overwhelming number of male shoppers. She silently observes, "It looks like fleet week and Whole Foods is the home port!"

Walking to her car and then placing her grocery sack in the trunk, she begins to replay the events that just took place. First there was the guy in produce, then the one in the dairy case, and finally the man at the check stand. Rita launches into uncontrollable laughter with the sad thought, "Has it really been that long since someone has shown me attention that I didn't even notice when I was getting hit on?" Sliding into the driver's seat, she pulls down the visor and proclaims boastfully, "Well, I guess you've still got it!"

CHAPTER 30

GRAVITY, SURPRISES, AND REALIZATIONS

Walking back from the restroom, Kathy is startled when she sees a few of the hospital's board members, along with the spokesperson for the hospital's merger, sitting together at a table having dinner. The emotions of the past few months and the frustration of how she and her staff have been treated begin to boil up inside her. Remembering the empowering words she and her friends spoke to Ali about standing up for herself and not letting her voice be silenced, Kathy decides to take her own advice and confront them. So with determination accompanying the wine running through her veins, Kathy marches over to their table with attitude in her every step. Not waiting for an invitation to join them, she abruptly sits down in one of the empty seats. Taking all of them by surprise, Kathy renders them speechless as she lets them know she has a few things to say about the board meeting earlier that afternoon.

After educating them on the right and wrong ways to manage employees, Kathy informs them that she will now be taking an active role in the merger, assertively setting times for them to meet early in the next week to discuss ways of making the transition of the merger move more smoothly as a whole. Once she feels her point has been made, she thanks them for their time and heads back to the book-club table, confidently knowing she did the right thing.

As Kathy nears the table, she can hear the conversation going on between her friends about the Sahara Desert in Sarah's pants and can't help herself from chiming in, "You know what they say—'Use it or lose it.'" Now seeing the table's eyes focus on her, she adds, "Hey, I am a nurse. I know what I am talking about." Climbing her way back to her perch in the center of the booth, she smiles, thinking about the night's events; one moment she is at a table talking about mergers and board members, and now she's at another, discussing the medical downfalls of accidental abstinence. "Man, I love book-club night!"

Rita quickly snarks, "Don't worry, Sarah. I'll gladly volunteer Jim."

"Gee, thanks," says Sarah with a wink.

Diane admits to her friends, as only women can, "Talking about losing it, the other day I caught a glimpse of myself in the mirror as I stepped out of the shower. What I saw shocked the crap out of me. There in the mirror were my grandmother's boobs staring back at me. They were like two empty gym socks, just hanging there. And let me just ask you, at what point did they decide to act in defiance and point downward? As much as I tried to arch my back, I couldn't for the life of me get these old girls to change their compass to face north."

Kathy educates the ladies. "You'll be happy to know that gravity doesn't just hate women. I saw Ed walking out of the bathroom the other morning. I swear his balls looked like they were knocking his knees. It was like watching the pendulum on an old grandfather clock. I couldn't look away. They were just swinging back and forth with each step. Back and forth, back and forth, it was mesmerizing and gross all at the same time."

"Oh, great, so this is what Ryan and I have to look forward to. What a great-looking couple we'll be, sitting around with our saggy, empty boobs and low-swinging balls," says Melissa in her most depressing voice.

Ali adds to the conversation, "It's not just the gravity that gets you. Has anyone else noticed graying in their southern regions? I mean, I am used to getting my roots dyed," she says as she points to her head. "But not my roots dyed," she finishes, pointing to her downtown lady parts.

"What? Are you kidding me? You can dye that?" questions Rita.

Bette reassures her, saying, "Oh, sure. I've been dyeing my landing strip since the early nineties. You've all heard the saying 'The rug should match the drapes.'"

Kathy giggles. "You mean, for those of you who still have rugs."

"Touché, my friend," replies Bette.

Melissa, sounding intrigued, comments, "Maybe I should try that. I wonder what Ryan would think about going to bed with a *redhead*."

Sarah, sounding completely defeated, adds, "Wonderful, one more thing for me to maintain in the off chance that I get lucky. That's just what I need. I finally get a guy that I want to sleep with, and just when things are going good, if you know what I mean, he goes downtown only to find a big white hair staring him in the face. I would be mortified!"

"Oh, ladies, you haven't a clue about what's mortifying," says Ali with the knowledge that no matter what the other ladies have experienced, nothing can compete with the most embarrassing night of her life.

"Sounds intriguing. Go on," says Diane with all her attention now directed toward Ali.

Pointing to Ali, Kathy says, "Look at the look on her face. Oh, this is going to be good." Then she orders, "Spill it, Ali!"

"Come on, Ali. I told you about the fruit snack between my legs," Sarah reminds her.

"Okay, okay, I farted," confesses Ali.

"Yeah, Ali, we all know. You fart all the time. We're used to it. It's just something you do," Diane says with compassion.

"No, you don't understand. I 'farted.'" Ali emphasizes her statement by using air quotes and then pauses before continuing her story, allowing each of the ladies to realize the monumental gravity of what she has just confessed.

"What? Ew!" says Melissa, laughing.

Bette says in disbelief, "No way!"

Pushing the inquiry, Rita asks, "Who were you with?"

Kathy interjects, "Now you have to tell us the story in detail." Then, adding insult to injury with a chuckle, she says, "Every little stinkin' detail."

"Well, since you asked me so nicely," replies Ali, while looking at Kathy. "You all remember Ken, right?"

"Isn't he the guy who dry heaved and made an embarrassing scene when you two were out to lunch at the Bayside and he found a hair in his lobster roll?" asks Bette. "Man, I wish I could have been there; it sounded hysterical!"

"That's the one," answers Ali.

"So he is a little squeamish. There's nothing wrong with that," says Sarah, defending his actions. "Everyone has their quirks. Who cares?"

"He's more than a little squeamish. I think neurotic would be more like it," quips Ali.

Ignoring Ali's reply, Sarah continues, "The more important thing is, don't you guys remember how hot he was? I know I could put up with a lot from a guy if he looked like that."

"Oh, you're right. He was hot," agrees Bette.

Rita adds to the conversation from what she remembers about Ken, "Yeah, you're right, Sarah. He was cute. And didn't he have a successful career, like a lawyer or dentist or something interesting like that?"

"I guess you could say that. He's a pilot," says Ali, answering their questions.

"That's right. I liked him. He seemed nice. Whatever happened to him? From the way you talked about him, I figured you two really hit it off," says Melissa.

Ali continues her tale of embarrassment. "We did hit it off, and I really liked him. Things were moving along nicely, and then came our third date. And everyone knows what happens on the third date. I had spent the afternoon grooming, tweezing, waxing, and choosing the right outfit. You know, the kind that said, 'Take me. I am ready and willing.' Anyway, after a romantic dinner at the Fork, we went back to my place for a drink."

Kathy chimes in, "I like where this is going. Continue."

Bette interjects, "All right already, get to the good stuff."

"Okay, okay. So we started making out in the living room and then moved the party to the bedroom. Things were going great. He was amazing. A few moments and positions later, I was on top, riding him like he was a bunking bronco, when all of a sudden I felt my stomach rumble."

"Oh no," Diane says with concern.

"I tried to ignore it, but it kept gurgling. I tried flexing my stomach in hopes of busting what might be bubbling up inside me, but no luck. I tried squeezing my butt cheeks while desperately attempting to keep the rhythm as I was moving up and down."

"Oh no," says Diane again with even more concern.

"When the gurgling wouldn't stop, I started to panic, and I could feel beads of sweat starting to form on my forehead. Knowing this wasn't going to end well, I let out a mumble of 'Oh God,' which Ken took as a compliment. So he started moving faster and faster. I closed my eyes, held my breath, and clinched so tight I thought I was going to pass out. He continued harder, faster, and even faster, until I couldn't hold it any longer, and for just a moment I relaxed my muscles. I mean, it was just a second, maybe even a nanosecond, but that's all the time it needed," she says, talking about her bowels as if they had a mind of their own. "They wouldn't be controlled. It was a total and complete mutiny of the most intimate kind."

"Oh no," insists Diane.

Defending herself, Ali says, "You don't understand. I needed to catch my breath. I thought I was going to pass out. So I unclenched for just a second. It was just for a quick second. I swear. And that, my friends, is when the unthinkable happened."

"You didn't!" exclaims Rita.

"I couldn't help it. I had been living off broccoli and cabbage. It wasn't my fault. It couldn't be stopped. All those smoothies, I didn't have a choice."

Sarah, with all the sympathy she can gather while grinning from ear to ear and trying desperately not to laugh, says, "Oh, sweetie, I am sure it wasn't that bad."

"It was as if a bomb filled with lethal gas had gone off. We were instantly engulfed in what can only be described as inhuman. I was so embarrassed that my body froze. When I finally mustered the courage to slowly open one eye and then the other, I found him staring back at me with a shocked expression plastered across his face. Within that moment, the once-bucking bronco I had strapped between my legs transformed from a stallion to a Shetland pony in a matter of seconds."

"Whoa," mumbles Kathy.

"So then, as I sat there, straddling him, not sure of what to do next, he looked at me and told me that he suddenly remembered he had an early-morning meeting and that he needed to be going home. With that announcement, he unceremoniously dumped me onto my side and leaped out of bed with the speed that would make Superman jealous. He pulled on his pants, slipped on his shirt, grabbed his shoes and coat, and left my apartment without any more explanation. Ladies, he didn't even take the time to slip on his shoes. He just grabbed his things and got out as fast as he could. Needless to say, I haven't heard from him since."

They all want to be supportive, but the story is too good. No one can contain her laughter. Sarah raises her glass and concedes. "You win, sister. Hands down, that was the worst date story of the night." She continues, "Your explosion makes my night with ferret boy look like a dream date. Well done, my friend, well done."

With her raised glass in hand and flushed cheeks, Ali joins in on the laughter consuming the table as Franc approaches the table joyfully carrying a martini, which she places in front of Sarah.

"Oh, I am sorry. I didn't order this," says Sarah, confused.

"I know. The gentleman at the bar had it sent over for you," Franc answers, grinning and adding a wink for emphasis.

Almost in unison, the ladies let out an over-the-top "Oooooh!"

"I hope he likes watermelon." Diane giggles.

Sarah, in her most mature demeanor, casually turns toward the bar to see who her secret admirer might be. Happily, she sees a nice-looking man with slightly graying temples looking in her direction. When their eyes meet, he smiles, nods, and raises his glass in a gesture that suggests "cheers." Sarah raises her martini in response and then turns back toward her friends. "Well, this is interesting," says Sarah with hope in her voice.

The fantasy of how the night may end for Sarah brings on a whole new discussion at the table regarding spur-of-the-moment encounters and questions of how she would explain the pungent, sweet smell of watermelons emitting from between her legs.

While the ladies continue to laugh and make fun of Sarah, Franc walks up to thank them for coming in tonight and then hands each of them their bill. Shocked by her appearance at the table, Ali looks at her watch and reports to the group that it is eleven thirty. Once again, they are surprised by how fast time has gone by. After each of the friends has paid her bill, they all move in one choreographed motion, collecting their unopened books, rising from the table, and leaving to hail cabs. All, that is, except for Sarah, who has decided to go to the bar to thank the nice gentleman for her drink in person.

The first cab pulls up to the front of the restaurant, and Melissa and Rita get in while the rest of the ladies wait together in the lobby for their cabs to arrive. The ride uptown gives Rita a chance to reflect on tonight's book club. After a night of listening to her friends Kathy and Melissa telling stories of the ways both Ryan and Ed support them and how Bette has found her true soul mate with Harry, Rita can't help but be reminded of all the good times she and Jim once had. She recalls how they started out as coworkers then became friends and later fell in love. Rita remembers how Jim used to tell the worst jokes, always forgetting the punch lines. He didn't care; he just wanted to see her smile. She thinks about how he cried at their wedding when they danced their first dance together as husband and wife, how he stayed up all night taking care of Rita and the boys when they came down with the flu while on vacation to the Berkshire Hills for Christmas, and how he remembers to bring her a dozen orange tulips on her birthday each year, knowing that they are her favorite flowers because they remind her of Sunday dinners at her grandmother's. These are real things, true things, and important things, things worth fighting for. At that moment, she lets her guard down and tells Melissa that she is still desperately in love with her husband and will do whatever it takes to save their marriage. Her vulnerability about her relationship with Jim is met with love, support, and a few tears from Melissa. Trying to be helpful, she offers to give Rita the name of a friend of hers who is a well-respected marriage counselor.

"Thank you. I think that sounds like a good place to start," replies Rita with a smile.

Kathy, Ali, and Diane have all left in their appropriate cabs, which makes Bette the last to leave the restaurant. Stepping out of the restaurant and into a waiting cab, Bette leaves book club tonight with a smile on her face. Somewhere between the drinks and desserts, a new book idea came to her. She may no longer be the voice for single ladies everywhere, but she realizes she still has plenty to say—staying true to who she is, a smart, fun, independent woman. She looks forward to exploring and introducing her readers to her new role as the voice of a savvy, confident, happily married woman. Getting into the cab, she gives the driver her address and tells him she is going home to see her husband.

━━◄┼ ┼►━━

En route back to their real worlds, each of the book-club friends is once again filled with the confidence to handle whatever life throws her way. Whether it is their careers, children, husbands, or hopes of finding Mr. Right, all of them take with them the knowledge that they are not alone. They will always have one another to lean on.

CHAPTER 31

AN EVENING AT FRANC'S COMES TO AN END

Derek is getting ready to leave for the night as he stops by the kitchen and takes a folded napkin from the breast pocket of his suit. Looking down at the young girl's phone number, he is flattered by her boldness and beauty. However, he knows his heart belongs to another. So without a second thought, he crumples the napkin and tosses it in the direction of the garbage can, unaware if he has hit his target or not. Pausing to gaze toward Franc's dark office, he says with a grin, "She's worth the wait." He then continues on his way, leaving through the back of the kitchen to his waiting car. Remembering the events of the evening, he is filled with the satisfaction of knowing Franc felt jealous today and is confident there's still hope for him to win her heart.

❦ ❧

In the dining room, the waitstaff is now clearing the ladies' empty table, knowing next month the booth will once again be filled with their laughter and friendship. A few choice quotes are quietly shared with giggles among the staff as they tell the bits of information that had escaped the not-so-soundproof banquette. This sense of joy that follows the book club's visit each month gives Franc pause to reflect on the restaurant's history with this special group of women. She has come to realize that book club is not about the books they read. It is about the support, unconditional love, and friendship between the members.

Back in her office, Franc completes the last of tonight's paperwork before taking a quick peek at the reservation book for the upcoming weeks. Looking over the book, she sees one entry that stands out from the rest. It's a reservation for five at eight o'clock on the last Thursday in May. Next to the reservation is a handwritten note by Sophia that reads, "*Celebrating a fifty-year-old challenge...I'll explain it to you tomorrow.*"

Confused and nervous, Franc cautiously questions, "Oh no. What does that mean?" Exhausted by the day's events, she closes the book and gathers her things to leave for the night. Crossing the kitchen, Franc is just hitting her stride when she passes the garbage bin and hears a crunching sound under her right foot. Stopping to collect the object in question, she is surprised at what she sees. Unraveling the discarded bundle, Franc realizes it's the piece of paper scribed with the tart's name and number, given to Derek earlier that evening. Franc can't help but smile at the thought of him tossing it into the garbage. Letting down her guard and giving in to her feelings, she thinks, "I may need to rethink my rule."

ABOUT THE AUTHOR

Novelist Jeannette Dashiell arms herself with humor, sass, and a tall glass of wine to tackle some of the most important milestones in a woman's life: dating, marriage, parenting, divorce, career, illness, tragedy, and the inevitable effects of time and gravity.
Dashiell discovered her love for writing after the untimely death of her oldest daughter, Hannah, in 2014. After being consumed with grief, Dashiell felt joy for the first time in months after waking from a dream about the unbreakable friendships among a group of women. Taking it as a sign to begin living again and with the support and encouragement from family, friends, and her own book club BABs "Books and Booze" (which Jeannette founded with her friends in 2006 and is still

going strong today) she began to write the story in her dream.

Jeannette Dashiell lives in Bellingham, Washington, with her husband Dennis and daughter Maddy.

9 781532 860294